SAME TIME, SAME MURDER

A GIL AND CLAIRE HUNT MYSTERY

ROBERT J. RANDISI
CHRISTINE MATTHEWS

WOLFPACK
PUBLISHING
— EST 2013 —

Copyright © 2018, 2005 Robert J. Randisi and Christine Matthews
All rights reserved.

Published in the United States by Wolfpack Publishing, Las Vegas.

Wolfpack Publishing
6032 Wheat Penny Avenue
Las Vegas, NV 89122

wolfpackpublishing.com

Paperback ISBN: 978-1-64119-459-4
Ebook ISBN: 978-1-64119-458-7

Library of Congress Number: 2018961772

For Ellen Burstyn and Alan Alda

AUTHORS' NOTE

There are some real people in this book. You'll recognize the names of other writers. We thought this would be fun. But there are no thinly veiled depictions of real people. If you think you see yourself, or someone you know, within these pages, you're wrong. Any resemblance the fictional characters in this book have to actual persons, living or dead, is purely coincidental. No, really.

SAME TIME, SAME MURDER

PROLOGUE

NO! No, no, no. The words slammed against the inside of her head with sledgehammerlike precision. There was pain in her head, and no sound in her ears except her beating heart. It was as if she were existing in a vacuum suddenly.

I can't look at this. Please, no. Don't make me look at this!

She covered her eyes.

Please . . . please . . . p . . . l . . . eeee . . .

But she had to look. It was as if she had no power over her own body. She pried her fingers apart, forced open her eyes.

Have to look. Maybe he's not . . . not . . . really . . . dead . . .

But there was so much blood. Thick, red, congealing there on the pink carpet. So much blood . . . How could he not be dead?

He was!

He was . . . dead.

The question hung in the air then: . . . Now what?

But before she could think any further, make any kind of

decision, there were people talking, shouting, crowding into the room, screaming. . . .

"Someone call the police! Hurry. Somebody call nine one one!"

"Who is that?" A man shoved her, and then another. In trying to get a look, they forced her closer to the dead man.

"Oh, my God. Is he dead?" one asked.

"Who are you?" the other man asked. "Did you see anything? Anybody?"

They were looking at her, but there was no accusation in their eyes. But there would be. . . .

I have to get out of here, her brain shouted. Get out! Run! Run, for Chrissake!

And then she was running. Running harder than she had ever thought she could.

Running.

Pushing.

Stumbling.

Couldn't stop.

Running until stomach cramps squeezed upward, burning her lungs, sending pain biting into her thighs. Running until she thought she would die!

Can't stop, her brain shrieked.

Run! Faster! Faster! Fasterfasterfaster . . .

CHAPTER 1

"SO? YA GOT THE ITCH?"

Claire looked across the room at her husband. "Oh no, don't you dare tell me you stepped in something that gave you a rash. We've planned this trip for months. You can't get sick. You can't! You know the rules—no getting sick on a vacation. Especially this—"

As Gil walked toward her, he held up his hands. "I was making a joke. You know, we've been married seven years? Isn't that supposed to be the time we get the itch to, ah, see if the grass is greener . . ."

"It's not a joke, Gil," Claire told him seriously. "I heard that they did a study—"

"Is this the same 'they' who did all those other studies?" he asked. "Like the one about coffee? Elixir of life—or death in a cup? And the one on wine? One glass with a meal keeps the heart pumpin', but two—or is it three?—are lethal? 'They're' always studying bats or pigs or drunken college students, trying to uncover a secret that will fix global warming, cure cancer, or magically remove ten years' worth of wrinkles."

She grabbed his face and kissed him deeply. Not just because she adored that face of his but mostly to shut him up. And when she released him, he had that dazed look in his eyes. Even after seven years of marriage. She playfully patted his cheek. She still had it.

"Next," she said. It was the signal that the subject had been closed. Move on. Get over it.

He smiled, stood there holding her for a moment, and then led her outside.

Their Knotty Pine Cabin was situated on a forested ridge near Devil's Pool in the Ozarks, at Big Cedar Lodge. They had gotten married in the fall, seven years ago today. It was the second marriage for both. And now in their forties, with all that youthful confusion and anxiety behind them, they both considered these to be the best years of their lives.

Claire inhaled deeply. "I love the autumn," she said as Gil deposited her into a worn Adirondack chair. "I know a lot of people think this time of year is sad. It gets gloomy and cold and everything dies, but I always think of it as a breather—a time-out."

Gil pulled a matching chair up beside her and stretched out. "I never thought of it that way, but you're right. Summer is always frantic—everyone expected to run and have fun."

"And it gets so hot in St. Louis," Claire said, "that I don't know why people even want to go outside when the humidity melts the life right out of them."

"Winter used to be the best. Until I got too old for snow-ball fights and had to shovel, scrape, and defrost. Spring, though, now spring's a beautiful time."

"Spring break," Claire moaned. "Spring break reruns all

year long on MTV, spring training, spring into action, spring cleaning."

Orange leaves drifted until caught in a gust and then were swept upward. When they finally landed, they covered the yellow and red ones, making the grass look as if it were a crazy quilt. November in Missouri was most often mild. Temperatures still climbed into the high seventies. But the air seemed more breathable. Instead of the heavy fragrance of cut grass or bushes loaded with roses, burning leaves, and smoke rising up from chimneys and fireplaces scented the crisp air. Hot dogs and hamburgers being grilled, fermenting apples, the first blast of heat from a furnace restarted after long summer days—all of it filtered through the trees and back to the couple.

"Happy anniversary, Claire." Gil reached out his hand.

She wove her fingers into his. "Happy anniversary, sweetie. Coming here was certainly one of your best ideas. It feels like we're all alone, lost in the woods."

She watched as he leaned to examine a pinecone. His red flannel shirt fit snugly, his hair was freshly cut, wispy around the ears and thinning on top. If someone had taken the time to look closely at the creases in his face, they would have said age complimented him.

"So," she asked, "do you want your present now?"

"I thought we'd wait until after dinner. Isn't Tucker taking us to Top of the Rock? He mentioned something about a new chef."

"You mean we have to wait almost the whole night?" she groaned.

Gil turned, hiding his grin. Disconnecting his hand from hers, he reached in a shirt pocket for the car keys. He wanted her to stew awhile and so took his time counting silently to ten. He had only made it to five when Claire spoke.

"Well, maybe you can wait, but I can't."

"Here you go, you big baby." He tossed her the keys. "Go look in the trunk."

Playing with the silver key chain, she pretended to be thinking very seriously about something. "No. You're right. We should wait until later."

"I hate when you do that."

"What? You hate when I admit you're right? You must be the only man in captivity who—"

"Claire, just go get the present."

She stood up. "If you insist."

Running to the car, she couldn't resist calling back to him over her shoulder, "After all, you are the boss around here."

"Tell me another one!" he shouted back.

When she returned, she was holding two packages. "Oh, look what I found in the trunk." Reading the name written across a small tag, she said, "and this one seems to be for someone named Sherlock." It had become one of her pet names for him ever since their first meeting at a mystery convention. "Is there a Sherlock here?"

"That would be me!" He raised his hand.

"Me first." Sitting back down in her chair, Claire turned the present over in her hands several times. The wrapping was red and metallic silver. A bunch of silk roses had been attached to the top.

"This is almost too pretty to open. Note the word: *almost*. And no card—very edgy, Gil. No one can say you're traditional."

"Just wait," he said. "The week's not over."

Carefully sliding her fingernail across the back, she

sliced through the tape and the paper fell gracefully into her lap. Opening the box, she stopped and stared down at the book enclosed. Lifting it up, she couldn't hide her excitement. The dust jacket had been doctored with one of her head shots from the studio. There she was, big as day, smiling back at herself. And in large white letters across the top was the title: *C Is for Claire,* instead of *C Is for Corpse,* as intended by its author.

"Where did you ever . . . I can't believe how thoughtful . . ."

"It's a first edition. The real cover's at home, so don't worry. And I had Sue Grafton sign it for you. Look on the title page." His excitement was always the best part.

Claire eagerly flipped the pages, stopping at the inscription. "C is for celebrate! Happy anniversary, Claire. Here's to seven more years of good things for you and that wonderful husband of yours. Love, Sue." She hugged the book to her chest, unable to look at Gil, sure that tears would spill down her cheeks. She hated being the emotional one. "I love it. Thank you."

"Now me?" he asked holding up his gift.

Claire nodded.

His present had been wrapped in children's birthday paper. Bugs Bunny and Daffy Duck were holding cakes and mugging it up. "Ah, you certainly know what I like, don't you?" He laughed. "And there's no card on this one, either."

"I know," she said. "It's spooky how alike we are."

"You still think it's spooky? By now, I think it's normal." He ripped the paper off, turning the large sheet into confetti. When he came to the box, he lifted the cover off and shouted, "All right! I was hoping you'd get the hint."

"How could I miss?" she asked. "For the last three months, you've been leaving catalogs all over the house.

And the red circle around item numbers—you're not very subtle, Gil."

Holding the boxed set up, he read, "'*Midsomer Murders.* Set in the seemingly benign villages of Midsomer County. Detective Chief Inspector Barnaby and his brash assistant, Sergeant Troy, find that bucolic charms hide a multitude of sins.'" Gil patted the box. "Ever since our last trip to England, I can't get enough of these British mysteries." Then, reading all the fine print on the side panel, he said, "Oh, Claire, these are DVDs."

"Really?"

"We can always exchange them for VHS."

The car keys came sailing back into his lap. "Maybe if you run your little self back to the car, you'll find the second half of your present in the backseat."

"A DVD player? But we both agreed we didn't need one, that our tapes are good enough."

Claire pulled her chair closer to his. "We don't *need* anything, Gil. As long as we have our life together, we don't need any of that other stuff. But I wanted you to have it. Just because. For fun, you know?"

"I know," he said, then kissed her.

CHAPTER 2

"SO," Tucker asked the couple sitting across from him, "didn't I tell you?"

Gil had only taken two bites of his steak, but from the appetizer to the salad to the main course, he had been impressed. "Delicious. Everything's great, Tuck."

"My trout is perfect," Claire said. "But you know me. The proof is in the—"

"Pudding? We have crème brûlée and a wonderful rice pudding with brandy sauce."

"You really love this place, don't you?" Gil asked. "It's great seeing you so happy."

"Not like the first time we met, huh, Gil?"

Claire had heard the story countless times. How on one particularly bright spring morning, Tucker Bowen had wandered into Gil's bookstore in University City, back home in St. Louis. Freshly divorced, unemployed, and displaced, he missed his kids, his friends, and the comfort of something—anything—familiar. Gil had recommended a few books, they'd talked, and their discussion led to lunch. That had been almost ten years ago.

"No." Gil shook his head. "Thank God for that. By the way, how's Reagan?"

"Good. She sends her regards. She really wanted to join us, but her mother's been ill."

"Don't you two have an anniversary coming up?" Claire asked.

"February. It'll be our fifth."

Gil sipped his wine and glanced at Claire, admiring how the flickering light from the fireplace made her blond hair sparkle.

"So, Claire, how does it feel being a big-time celebrity?" Tucker asked. "Reagan loves watching you on that home-shopping show of yours."

She laughed. "I wouldn't know about the 'big-time,' but I do love my job."

"And she's damn good at it," Gil chimed in. "According to the latest stats, her morning show is the most popular on the network."

"We're both lucky guys, Gil," Tucker said thoughtfully. "I don't know how, but we managed to convince two great ladies to marry us." He raised his wineglass. "One more toast."

Gil and Claire put down their silverware and went for their glasses. "This is the last one, Tuck. Okay?" Claire said.

"Promise." Then, looking more solemn than he had all evening, Tucker said, "To love."

"To love!" Gil said enthusiastically.

"To love," Claire repeated, then took a sip from her glass.

After drinking, Tucker looked at Claire. "Do I detect a note of cynicism?"

"Well . . ." she began.

"Claire always insists that men are more romantic than women. I don't think it's true, though," Gil said.

Claire lowered her knife and raised an eyebrow. "Oh come on! Tuck, you've known Gil almost as long as I have. I remember how he plotted to match you up with Reagan. Admit it: He's a hopeless romantic."

"Just because I wanted to see a friend happy? That makes me romantic?"

"She's right, Gil. You *are* a sap for all that stuff. How many times have you seen *The Bridges of Madison County*?"

"Clint Eastwood. I've seen all his movies."

"And *Somewhere in Time*?" Tucker asked. "You were the one who recommended it to Reagan and me."

"The Grand Hotel! I had just been out there and thought you'd enjoy the scenery."

"I told you so," Claire said smugly. "I'm not the only one who's noticed this flaw in your personality."

"Terminal romanticism. Okay, I guess there could be worse things." Tucker reached across the table to pat Gil's shoulder. "Never change, buddy. The world needs more like you out there."

The threesome had finally finished their entrees and were trying to decide on dessert, when Tucker remembered news he had meant to share with his friends. "Oh, I almost forgot, and Claire, maybe even you will be excited."

Claire adjusted her velvet scarf. "What?"

"Reagan is writing a book."

Gil sat back in his chair. "Is she still freelancing? Her travel pieces are some of the best I've read."

"Given everything up until this book is finished."

"Wow. So, what's it about? Tell us all the details." Claire didn't consider Reagan Bowen one of her closest friends, but that wasn't from a lack of interest. The two women maintained such busy schedules and their work resulted in them having different lifestyles. When Claire was on the air, Reagan was sleeping. When Reagan was eating a late supper, Claire was getting ready for bed. The few lunches they had managed to share had always been enjoyable. Claire considered Reagan her "artsy" friend and envied the free-spirited way she approached everything.

"It's called *Love at First Sight,* or at least that's the working title. She's gathered stories about how people met, fell in love, and married. Kinda corny, huh?"

"I'd read it," Claire said. "And we both know Gil would love it."

"So it's nonfiction?" Gil asked. "A series of essays?"

"I think of it more as a sort of factional romance."

"Has she always been interested in those kinds of stories?" Claire asked.

"As long as I've known her. She's got some great ones, too. There's this couple who met during the war. The woman's best friend was set up on a blind date but at the last minute got chicken pox. So Mary goes to meet the guy— a soldier—at a dance to tell him the date's off. They start talking, fox-trot to some Glenn Miller, and the next thing you know they're in love."

"Nice," Gil said. "You hear about a lot of those things happening during the war."

"But here's the best part," Tucker continued. "The guy's getting shipped out and asks Mary to go with him to the train station to say good-bye. He's planning to propose, but she thinks it'll be the last time they'll ever see each other."

"Train stations," said Claire, sighing. "Now that's a romantic image."

Gil agreed.

"She shows up in her best dress," Tucker told them, "white gloves, one of those little hats they wore back then. There're all these soldiers rushing around, porters loading up bags, trains chugging up and down the tracks. The two of them stand kissing, she's crying, and he pops the question in the middle of all the commotion."

"And she says yes," Gil added.

"No."

"She's afraid he'll get killed in combat?" Claire asked.

"No. She wasn't quite in the right place, in her heart, as he was. She came from a large family, had never left her hometown, so it all seemed too soon and too foreign."

"Some love story," Gil grumbled.

Tucker folded his hands on the table. "The guy is crushed. He pushes the ring deep into his pocket, gets on the train. His buddies are all talking and laughing, but he just sits there. Mary is waving good-bye, but he doesn't even look at her.

"Finally, the soldier next to him asks what's wrong and he spills his guts. His buddy spreads the word, and pretty soon all the men are hanging out of the windows, shouting at the poor girl to say yes. 'Come on, marry him!'

"The excitement spreads down the line and now they're all shouting, 'Say yes! Say yes! Say yes!' They're stamping their feet, clapping their hands; even people standing on the platform get into the act. 'Say yes! Say yes!' "

"I love this!" Claire said.

"So the train starts to pull out of the station and Mary starts crying. She says she loves him but that she's afraid. Everyone's shouting, 'Say yes!' "

"And she does?" Gil asked.

Tucker nodded. "All the soldiers reach out, dozens of

hands grab for her, and together they pull her up and through the window into the train."

"How far did she ride with them?"

"They got married at the next stop, he came back from the war all in one piece, and they eventually celebrated more than fifty years together."

Gil blew out a long sigh. "Are all the stories that exciting?"

"No." Tucker said. "Some are tender; some are sad."

"Well, I can hardly wait to read the book when Reagan's finished. Tell her I volunteer my services as a proofreader."

"She'd love that, Claire."

They ordered a local treat, blackberry cobbler à la mode, and champagne for dessert. And after they finished stuffing themselves, Tucker asked, "So, tell me, how did you two meet?"

"I'm sure I told you," Gil said while wiping vanilla ice cream from the corner of his mouth.

"Refresh my memory."

"Oh," Claire said, "it's a long, complicated story. And I'm sure that if Gil told you—and he's told everyone—you'd remember."

Tucker smiled. "So, what was the most memorable thing about your first meeting?"

"Robin Westerly."

"He was the guest of honor at the convention where I met Claire," Gil said.

"And Claire had a crush on him? Something like that?"

"No." Claire said. "He got himself killed."

"Now I know I haven't heard this story before."

"Got a week?" Gil asked.

CHAPTER 3

"KILLED?" Tucker Bowen looked shocked. "A week? Not this visit, but I can give you a few hours. How about we go over to the lounge at the Devil's Pool and have a few drinks? At least you can get started. This would make a great chapter for Reagan's book. Would that be okay? I could take a few notes. Hey, if you give me a minute, I can run out to my car and get a recorder. Better yet—"

Claire looked anxiously at Gil. "Wait a minute. Tuck, I don't think the station would like any more publicity focused on my private life. After that whole thing a few years ago with the stalker, all the headlines . . . I almost lost my job. No, definitely not. I've been trying to keep a low profile."

"But this is about love." Tucker smiled.

"No," Claire said. "Our story is mostly about murder."

"And I certainly don't want tourists coming to the store just to gawk at me," Gil said. "I know you two think I'm charming and wonderful, but to strangers hearing our story, I'd be just another stop on their way through St. Louis: The Arch, the riverboats, Forest Park, and the lovesick bookstore owner who solved a murder. Besides," he continued, "it was all over the papers years ago and I still get comments."

Tucker thought the two were being overly cautious, but he didn't voice his opinion. Instead, he said, "Okay, so just tell me the story. From two friends to another. No publicity, no book deal."

"Forgive us if we sound like prima donnas," Gil said, "but we had a few bumpy years when we started out together, and now things have finally calmed down a bit."

"I wouldn't hurt you two for anything," Tucker said. "So will you just please—no strings attached—tell me the story?"

Big Cedar Lodge was furnished with custom-crafted items. Artisans from all over the country had been commissioned, and next to Disney properties, Big Cedar and its various resorts employed more craftsmen than any other company. That's why when Claire entered the comfortable lounge, she was overwhelmed not only by its beauty but by all the work that was evident in every tiny detail: from the chande-liers—hand-carved, adorned with copper miniatures of local animals—to the huge fireplace constructed of local lime-stone. The overstuffed love seats, covered in navy blue tapestry, were arranged around large oak coffee tables. A huge deer's head was mounted above the fireplace, and while she had never liked such things, it did look perfect. The smell of cedar chips wafted across the room as the fire-place crackled, and the spice candles scattered throughout created an almost enchanted place to begin their story.

After they ordered brandy and had settled back, Gil began.

"It was a dark and stormy night."

"Oh Gil. I don't believe you! You'll use any opportunity to stick that horrible line in somewhere!"

"Tucker, it was a beautiful weekend in May—bright, cool, just lovely. Come on, Gil, tell it right."

He winked at Tucker. "She'll end up telling more of this than I will. Guaranteed."

Claire crossed her legs. "Well, I was living in Omaha at the time. Several years before, I had read a book, which became one of my favorites: *The Mirror,* by Marlys Millhiser."

"That's one of Reagan's favorites, too," Tucker said, amazed. "Apparently, a lot of women loved it, because I was at a fundraiser one evening and met a woman who later became one of my best friends. We were discussing books and she mentioned *The Mirror.* "

"And I was in Omaha as a book dealer for a mystery convention to be held at one of those huge Holiday Inns, the kind with the pool in the middle, under a dome," Gil said.

"So my friend Donna reads in the paper that there's going to be a mystery convention in town and Marlys Millhiser is listed as one of the authors attending.

"We got so excited, just like two teenagers planning to descend on the Beatles. We both dug out a copy of the book and decided we would go to the convention, determined to meet Marlys and get an autograph."

"Do you know this author?" Tucker asked Gil.

He nodded. "She's great. But maybe if she'd known that these crazy people were planning to attack her—"

"Attack?" Claire sounded indignant. "We only wanted to tell her how much we loved the book and ask if we could please buy her a drink or lunch—something in appreciation."

"And did you?"

"We took our positions in the bar—you know how writers like to drink; at least that's what we'd heard. So we were sitting there and Marlys walked in. We only had the photo on the dust jacket of the book to go on, and that was almost ten years old."

"And the name tag," Gil added.

"It was under her jacket."

Tucker realized the couple had been right. At this rate, it would take a week to hear their story. "Why don't you skip ahead to the part where you two first met?"

CHAPTER 4

IT NEVER LEFT HIM: how close he'd come to losing her back then at the very beginning, it had almost been their ending. He'd thought he was so desensitized, what with all the news footage he'd watched: executions with dinner, bombings for lunch, murders and rape with breakfast. Movies, reality TV, horror stories passed down from parent to son.

"I once knew a guy who chewed his fingernails and then swallowed them. Years and years of eating all those nails," his father once told him. "And you know what happened? He died before his sixteenth birthday. No one could figure out what happened. Jack ran track; everyone loved that kid. But when they opened him up, there were all those sharp little nails stuck to his insides like pins in a cushion. See? You gotta be careful," his father warned. "Life will kill ya, son."

But an honest-to-God dead body. Not all clean and antiseptic like in a funeral home—flowers, music, refreshments in the back. He'd always had time to prepare as he walked from the parking lot to the front door.

But that day, all those years ago . . . it felt more as if it all had happened only a few hours ago.

The blood, pooled under the dead man's head. One bullet to that bald head. Thank God the damaged part had been pressed against that god-awful pink carpet. Pink . . . how he hated pink, and mauve—almost every hotel room back then had come wrapped in that horrible mauve.

The image had stayed with him; he couldn't shake it, especially now, talking about how he'd first met Claire. One of his favorite stories always had to come with that kicker.

A dead guy. A not so very nice guy. An arrogant son of a bitch, in fact. But he hadn't deserved to die that way. Laid out like that—on display—strangers gawking.

Gil had wanted to run away and hide until the mess was all cleaned up. But what would Claire have thought of him then, when he'd been trying so hard? He'd had to stand there. He'd had to.

No matter how he rearranged the facts, the horror of it was always back there, telling him, It could have been you, son. It could have been any one of you. Life will kill you if you don't watch out.

He pushed down the image and hoped that even in his dreams the fear would never come out for Claire to hear.

CHAPTER 5

HER LAST NAME had been Duncan back then; she had been married to Frank for fourteen years. She once told someone that if she ever wrote her autobiography, she'd call it *Everything I Never Wanted To Be and More*. She had had a nice house, two cars in the garage, a dog, a yard, even the white picket fence. But except for her son, Paul, she hadn't wanted any of it. Her father once asked why she wasn't happy. After all, he'd told her, she had what every woman wanted. Claire often wondered where her father, the most chauvinistic man she'd ever known, had gotten this great insight into women's hearts. But she'd never asked him.

When she thought back to that afternoon, she always remembered Gil Hunt as being larger than anything human she'd ever known before. Not in the physical sense. It was his personality. His voice, his laugh. His soul. He would forever claim he'd been drunk that day and could not be held responsible for anything he might have said or done. But she knew he used that as a defense, a way to cover his nervousness.

"Marlys, can I buy you a drink?" Gil had asked as he

approached the small table she shared with Claire and Donna.

"Got one, thanks," She held up her glass.

"Well then, can I buy you lovely ladies anything?"

Lovely ladies. She thought that expression lived somewhere between corny and old-fashioned. She liked it.

"No thanks," the women said in unison.

"Okay, no drinks. How about an introduction, then?"

After names were exchanged, Gil sat on a stool across from Claire and studied her, all the while talking . . . entertaining. He made them laugh with stories about his beloved New York City. He was funny and charming. Gil Hunt and Claire Duncan liked each other from the start. . . . Well, they found each other interesting.

Almost everyone who passed through the bar stopped by the table to talk to Gil. He knew authors, book dealers, editors, and publishers, as well as the bartenders and waitresses. She found out he'd been attending mystery conventions for years.

He thought she was pretty. He mentioned it at the time and often throughout the next few days. He found her charming, funny, and smart. Weeks later, he realized he couldn't even remember what her friend Donna looked like. But Claire—blond, green-eyed Claire—he remembered. He said she glowed.

Their conversation started off light and easy and stayed that way. Each of them was married. Each had children—he had two boys and she had one. Both were in their thirties and wise enough to know nothing could come of their meeting. Not that year. Not then. "So, are you girls going to the banquet tonight?" Gil asked.

"I'm heading home," Marlys said. "Family business."

"We got tickets weeks ago," Donna said. "Can't come to

one of these things and not go all the way." Donna was always throwing out suggestive lines.

"Well," Gil said, "I'd love to sit with you, but I've got to give a speech. I'm this year's toastmaster. Maybe I'll see you later."

"Maybe," Claire said.

And that was about it.

"What about the murder?" Tucker asked.

"There was only sexual tension that first year," Gil said, smiling at Claire.

"Well, maybe for him." She nodded toward her husband. "Sorry, hon, but you seemed more a curiosity than an object of desire."

"Fine," he said playfully. "I guess my boyish charm didn't work on you right away."

"'Boyish charm'?" Tucker asked.

"Gil takes great pleasure in reminding me I'm the elder one in this relationship. Only by three years, though. And at our age, I don't think three years' difference matters to anyone."

"I'm her boy toy." Gil smiled broadly.

"Too much information," Tucker said. "How about you get back to your story?"

Claire began. "The next year, I was anxious to attend the convention because of friends I had made the year before. I was working for a local news station and they wanted me to do a few author interviews. And . . . well, I was wondering if I might see Gil around."

"I had been through a horrible year," Gil said. "Got divorced; my books and I were living—*existing* is a better word—in a basement apartment in St. Louis. The bookstore was limping along. My father had died suddenly, so I was flying back and forth to New York to help my mother out. I got depressed, lost a lot of weight. I was not a happy guy. But work kept me busy, and I was looking forward to the convention in Omaha. The hotel was close to the racetrack —it's gone now, but it was fun spending time watching the horses."

"And so you guys saw each other across a crowded room and love bloomed?" Tucker asked.

"No. Truth is, we didn't see each other until the last day —just about the last hour," Claire told him.

"I had been busy and felt that the year before I might have been a little . . ."

"Drunk?" Claire asked.

"Well, maybe a little tipsy, and I was embarrassed. And I looked and felt like I'd been run over by a train. Definitely not the best time of my life."

"So, I'm getting ready to leave after spending three days in and out of the hotel. I see a man who I think is Gil, but he's too thin and doesn't even look at me. At first, I think I'm mistaken, and then I realize it's him."

"I felt lousy."

Tucker looked down at his drink. The amber liquid clung to the side of the glass. After taking a gulp, he turned to Gil. "I wish I'd known things were so bad for you back then. I feel awful."

"Come on," Gil said. "We'd only met about a year before. It wasn't as if we were that close."

"Even if you had been," Claire said, "he wouldn't have mentioned a thing. It's taken me years to loosen this guy up."

Gil slapped Tucker on the shoulder. "Those days are long gone. History. But thanks for the thought."

"Anyway," Claire continued, trying to lighten the mood, "I'm getting ready to walk out of the hotel lobby and I see this man slink across the room. I can't resist and yell, 'Gil! Gil Hunt!' He stops and waves a pathetic little wave."

"Being the shy, demure woman she is, Claire walked over to me and asked if I'd been avoiding her. I was stunned. She was so . . . direct."

"Because it was true. You *were* avoiding me. And I made you admit it."

Tucker sat back straight in his chair. "Remind me not to try to hide anything from you."

Gil waved to the waitress to bring the trio another round. "I tried to think of a way to make it up to her, especially after looking into those beautiful green eyes again. So I told her I'd take her to dinner a year from that day. I grabbed a piece of paper and wrote, 'May twenty-eighth, seven o'clock. Be there. Aloha, Gil.' "

"Aloha?" Tucker laughed. "Is that code for something?"

"I wondered, too," Claire said, "but he thought he was being clever referring to the traditional closing line of *Hawaii Five-O*. After he gave me the note, I told him to write himself one so he wouldn't forget."

"Bet you didn't know how pushy Claire can be, huh?"

"I was playing with you. And you didn't tell Tuck it had been a bad year for me, too. I was separated, my airtime was getting less frequent, and my mother had died."

"So I wrote a note to myself and we said good-bye. I went home and hung it on a bulletin board in the kitchen."

Claire laughed. "I put mine on a bulletin board in my office."

"And I thought that whatever happened during the next year, no matter how bad things got," Gil said, "at least I had that meeting to look forward to."

CHAPTER 6

"COME ON," Tucker moaned, "Reagan is going to kill me. This story is too good to waste."

"Waste?" Claire wondered at the choice of word.

Gil looked sternly at his friend. "We told you—"

"I know, I know. Privacy and all that, but forget about publication. It's just that Reagan loves these kinds of things. Fate. Soul mates. All this love stuff."

Claire looked at Gil. "Well, maybe . . ."

"Good, we'll all have dinner tomorrow. You're staying for the whole week, right?" Tucker asked.

"Yes," Gil said.

"I'll have the kitchen send over one of their special baskets. They'll pack everything we'll need: steaks, salad, wine, the works. They'll even start up the grill. All we'll have to do is throw the meat on the fire and enjoy."

"Sounds perfect," Claire said. "How very lucky for us that our friend here knows the territory."

"So, tell us, how goes the digging?" Gil asked. "You haven't told us anything about what brought an important archaeologist such as yourself out here this time."

Tucker looked embarrassed. "Oh, technically I'm an engineer."

Claire smiled. "And a modest one at that."

"Sam Crockett, the horticulturist on the property here, found something interesting over near Devil's Pool. Quite a history out in this part of the country. The Osage tribe moved into the Ozarks and used the White River region for their hunting grounds around the thirteenth century," Tucker explained as he tried to pay the tab. "Sorry I have to cut this short, but they're holding a room for Reagan and me over at Valley View Lodge."

Gil pulled out his wallet. "It'll be great to see her again; it's been quite a while."

The focal point of their cabin was a large four-poster bed covered with a luxurious spread woven in warm earth tones. A triangular stained-glass window, artfully placed at the peak of the A-framed ceiling, added quiet elegance. As the couple sank deep into the soft mattress, they rolled into each other's arms.

"Telling our story tonight was almost as good as living it," Claire said.

"I was thinking the same thing."

"I wish we could get back some of the newness."

"Not me." Gil sighed. "I was so frightened all the time, at the beginning. Afraid we wouldn't work out. Afraid you'd wake up one morning and think you'd made a horrible mistake being with me."

Claire kissed him tenderly on the cheek. "We're stuck with each other, I'm afraid."

"Sounds like a good deal to me." He wrapped his arms

around her. "So, after reviewing the past years, you're happy enough to sign up for another seven?"

"I'll get back to you in the morning."

His card was propped against her cosmetic bag. She smiled to herself as she opened it. The couple on the front were somewhere between sixty and death. They were holding hands, standing on a beach, staring out at the ocean. It was a silly take on those romantic greeting cards showing beautiful Italian women gazing up seductively at a handsome dark man. Gil always said those were made for people too young and inexperienced to know what real love was about. But this? This couple in their too-tight swimsuits showing too much wrinkled skin. Across the blank inside, Gil had written, "Till death or high tide do us part."

"Claire," Gil shouted from the bedroom, "I don't believe you got me the same card!"

She turned off the bathroom light and went back out to the bedroom, where he was sitting on the sofa, holding a cup of coffee in one hand and her card in the other.

"Why are you surprised?" she asked. "I thought you were used to it by now."

"I know." He laughed, "But sometimes it still feels creepy. It's as if you're walking around in there." He pointed to his head.

"Well, I may have gotten the same card, but I didn't write the same thing inside."

"No, yours was much more poetic." Standing up, he held the card in front of him like a hymnal and read the words as seriously as he could. "'When we are older, losing our minds, many years from now, I will still be watching you sell those books, eat your pasta, give me those looks.

Women get better, sexier, too. So if you're real good, play your cards right, I will stay with you . . . forever.'"

He looked at her as if she were crazy. "You're weird."

She shrugged.

"Just the way I like my women."

It was another gorgeous day in paradise. A mild wind gusted by every now and then. The gourmet basket Tucker had promised arrived, complete with two waiters, at 4:30 that afternoon. By five o'clock, as Reagan and Tucker pulled up, the coals were perfect and the wine was chilled.

Reagan, her dark hair short and spiked in that bohemian way Claire envied, wore her favorite black boots, comfortable jeans, an orange sweater, and a fleece jacket printed with horses in brown and cream. Tucker was dressed more casually than Claire had ever seen before. His jean jacket was slightly frayed around the cuffs and the Yankee baseball cap looked like he actually wore it often.

"Claire," Reagan said, "I love that jacket. Is it new?"

Claire rubbed her hand along the soft leather sleeve. "Gil gave it to me for our last anniversary."

"He certainly has good taste."

Gil pulled on the collar of his shirt. The print was copied from the painting of dogs seated around a poker table, smoking and playing cards. "I sure do!"

"Oh Gil," Tucker said in his best falsetto, "I love that shirt. It's so cute."

Reagan patted the chair next to hers, signaling Claire to sit. "Ignore them. Let's get right to the good stuff. Tuck got me all caught up in your story. He was so psyched when I got back to the room last night."

"Maybe we should wait until we're finished eating," Gil said.

"You can start now. Please. Take your time. Don't leave one thing out." Reagan settled back to watch Gil cook the steaks. "I like mine rare, Gil."

"When Gil cooks, everything comes out medium," Claire warned.

"That's fine, as long as he tells the story," Reagan said.

Tucker stood by Gil. "I'll supervise. Isn't that what friends are for?"

"Hey, friend," Gil said, "you paid for dinner. It's your party; I'm just here to serve and obey."

"God, Claire." Reagan winked. "You've trained him well."

"It sure wasn't easy."

"Here we go," Gil moaned. "She's going to tell you I didn't show up for our first date, but I was there, sitting right next to the cowboy."

CHAPTER 7

AS SHE GOT DRESSED, she wondered what the hell she was doing. He wouldn't be there—the convention wasn't scheduled to start until the next day. What made her think he would come in early just to have dinner with her?

She'd already changed her clothes three times. Nothing too sexy. On a first date, that could translate into slutty. And she certainly didn't want him to think of her as too businesslike. Her favorite skirt never let her down; it was just the right length and the material lay in flattering folds. A simple black blouse. Not too revealing, but feminine. Not too feminine, no ruffles or bows. She hated bows.

Grabbing a jacket, she looked at the note he had written the previous year. The corners were pierced with tiny holes. How many times had she taken it off the bulletin board, read it, and replaced it? Silly. The whole thing was silly. But oh so *very* exciting.

She looked up the number for the hotel and dialed. "Do you have a Gil Hunt registered?" she asked, wondering if his full name was Gilbert. Why was she doing this?

When the operator confirmed Gil was there, she felt

those damn butterflies skittering around in her stomach again.

"No, I don't want to be connected. Thanks."

On the way to the hotel, she wondered again if he had actually come to town a day early just to keep their dinner date. No, he probably had to get his books set up in the dealers' room. All that packing and unpacking, arranging, it must take quite a few hours to get things right, she thought. More than likely, he had forgotten all about that silly note long ago.

It was exactly seven o'clock when she parked her car in front of the Holiday Inn. After turning the keys, she sat there a moment. So, what's the worst thing that can happen tonight? she asked herself. I'll see him and he won't remember me. And I'll feel like a fool. And I'll go home. Okay, act like a grown-up. Whatever happens, you're not going to die. She got out of the car.

Ten minutes later, when he still hadn't shown up, she walked across the lobby and into the lounge. It was a quiet evening: A couple sat at a corner table; four men were sitting at the bar. She realized she didn't know Gil well enough to recognize him from the back. Having been born and raised in Chicago, her first impulse was to shout, "Hey! Gil! Paging Gil Hunt!" But she suppressed the urge.

Okay, she thought, process of elimination. The guy at the very end of the bar was too heavy. The cowboy wearing the large black hat on the other end was definitely not Gil. A man sat beside the cowboy, talking to the bartender, calmly sipping his drink. If that was Gil, why would he be here in the bar instead of in the lobby, waiting for her? The fourth guy suddenly turned and hopped off his stool. Definitely not Gil.

She walked back to the lobby.

The house phone! She called up to his room. The phone on the other end rang and rang . . . and rang.

By 7:30, she realized she was very hungry, and disappointed and angry at herself for thinking he had taken the date as seriously as she had.

She started to leave, when she remembered his note in her pocket. Walking to the front desk, she scribbled a message across the paper: "I was here—you weren't. Now you're gonna pay." She signed it and then, after a moment spent debating with herself, wrote her phone number across the bottom. Evidence she had been there. The tone, playful . . . hopefully. Why was she doing this? She gave it to the desk clerk and headed out to get some dinner.

He'd lost the note. But there he was in Omaha on the twenty-eighth day of May. At least he knew he had that right. He checked into his room and called down to the front desk to check for messages. None.

After unpacking, he went downstairs to get some lunch. No, he was too nervous to eat. What the hell was he doing? Married all those years, now newly divorced, it was time to enjoy just . . . being. And Claire seemed fun and adventurous, making him write that note for himself. Damn, damn, where had he put it? He'd gone through everything at home —his new home, actually, the tiny basement apartment he found he was liking so much.

Oh, stop it, he told himself. She probably didn't even remember the date, or him, either, for that matter. Why should she?

He went and checked out the dealers' room. He hadn't brought as much stock as other times. This year felt different, for some reason. Besides, he wanted to have more time to spend with friends, both old and . . . new. He wanted to have fun, and relax.

It only took a few hours to get everything unpacked and set up. He stopped to talk to several friends and then hurried upstairs to take a shower. His plan was to start waiting for her at five o'clock. He was sure he wouldn't have asked her to dinner any earlier than that.

He was wearing a new suit. His tie had an abstract design of red and blue cubes. He checked his mustache and beard, patted down a stray hair near the nape of his neck. He wasn't usually this fussy about his appearance. Satisfied, he hurried back downstairs to wait.

He wondered where everyone was; it was so quiet. Sitting there on that long black vinyl-covered sofa, he wondered if anyone was dumb enough to think it was leather. He straightened his tie, crossed his legs, uncrossed them. Half an hour crawled by.

"Yo, Gil," he heard someone yell. "What're you up to all by yourself here in the lobby?"

Before he turned, he recognized his friend Michael's voice. "Nothing, just waiting."

"Got plans for dinner?"

Gil checked his watch again. It was 5:35. "I hope so."

"Must be someone special, to make you put on a suit," Michael observed. "How about one drink while you wait?"

Conversation would make the time pass more quickly. "Okay. Just one."

Several TV screens had been set up on either end of the

small bar. Instead of sports, they televised Keno games. The two friends decided to play a few cards while they visited, and the next thing Gil knew, it was 6:30.

"Looks like you been stood up, buddy." Michael swallowed the last of his beer. "A bunch of us are heading down to Ross's. They're supposed to have the best steaks in town. Why don't you come along?"

"I have to check something first," Gil said.

Walking into the lobby, he looked for Claire. He walked down the hall leading to the dealers' room. He checked another small bar tucked away by the pool. Realizing he didn't remember her last name, he suddenly felt foolish for even thinking she would meet him that night.

Returning to the bar, he told Michael he'd join him.

"Wait here. I'll go round everyone up."

Gil took a seat next to a cowboy at the bar. It was 6:55.

"Hit anything?" the man asked, pointing to the Keno game.

"No, nothing," Gil said. As he sat there, he couldn't stop thinking about Claire, and at the same time marveled at his own naiveté.

It took half an hour for Michael to return. By the time he did, Gil was starving. As the group headed toward the lobby, Gil made one last quick check, walking down the hall, past the gift shop, and then met his party outside at 7:40.

Gil had served the salad while the steaks were cooking on the grill. Since he had been doing most of the talking, he was a little behind the others in eating.

"Well, don't stop there," Reagan pleaded as Gil poked a forkful of salad into his mouth.

"I think Claire should take it from here," he said after swallowing. "Wow, this salad is great."

Reagan looked at her husband, who was also chewing vigor-ously, then at Claire, who, for the moment, seemed lost in thought.

CHAPTER 8

SHE HAD NEVER TOLD GIL.

The murder part was coming up. She hated telling that part. At the beginning of their relationship, she'd had nightmares—lots of them. Blood-soaked, horrific. And still she had never told Gil about any of them. Poor guy, he'd only feel he'd contaminated her in some way.

Now there were unexpected flashbacks, as well as nightmares. White skin—porcelain. Stillness—the room noisy, frantic, but underneath it all, a void. Black—blood appearing black, soaking into that hideous carpet beneath the body. A murder scene on a cop show, and she was back in Omaha at warp speed, eight years earlier. An interview on the news with a detective, his calm voice repeating facts over and over, and she was in the police station again, frightened, gripping Gil's hand with everything in her.

"Fear is ignorance." Hadn't Truman said it first? And then her second-grade teacher, her mother, her father, her philosophy professor, Dr. Phil.

Murder had frightened her beyond anything she'd ever experienced. But she wasn't stupid. Murder meant death.

Death meant no longer living. And she had counseled herself that she had every right to be afraid, in spite of knowing all the details. She'd been thrust into a frightening situation; it was only natural that she would be frightened.

But nightmares about murder soon gave way to a different variety.

Seeing him like that, spread out on the pink carpet, blood spilling out of his head. She'd had a front-row seat to an event that should have been sacred.

Waiting for the police, she took in all the details. His toupee, lying across the room, looking like a hairy tarantula. He'd been so particular about concealing his shiny head, and now he was grossly exposed. Not only his head but his body. A damp towel was wrapped around his thick middle and some of the people were actually giggling, saying how fat he looked.

We're going to rot in hell. All of us, she thought.

But I didn't point or laugh, she told herself. I didn't even smile. The dialogue in her head ping-ponged back and forth. Some nights it woke her as she tossed from side to side.

But you looked. You stared. You could have walked away, showed the man some respect. Instead, you stayed and gawked.

I'm a horrible person!

Scrooge laying on his deathbed, in *A Christmas Carol*. Now *those* women were horrible. Pulling at the bed curtains, the blankets, running off to sell them to scum in a back alley.

That poor man. Having to endure the humiliation.

The nightmares showcased her now biggest fear—dying in public. Strangers staring at her. She helpless—at the mercy of their thoughts, their laughter, their ridicule. Dropping to her knees slowly, clutching her chest. No one notic-ing. Then hitting the pavement hard. Her nose crunching into the concrete. Hundreds of legs walking over her, around her. Lying there, humiliated, undignified, silly. No one helps me. Not one single person helps me.

She'd kept the dreams to herself. Gil was never in any of them.

CHAPTER 9

"I CAN'T STAND IT!" Reagan screamed, snapping Claire from her unwanted reverie. "This has all the suspense of a made-for-TV movie."

"Yeah, well, we'll have to put it on pause for a minute," Gil said. "The steaks are ready. Claire, honey, can you bring me some plates?"

She grabbed two of the four dishes she'd found in their rustic kitchen. "I hope you didn't burn mine too badly. You know I like my steak medium rare, really, but I'll settle for anything as long as it's not burned. Gee, I just realized how hungry I am."

Tucker distributed the baked potatoes. "Everyone hurry up and do something so we can sit down and eat. Gil and Claire can continue to entertain us during dinner."

"Thanks," Claire said as she set Tucker's steak down in front of him. "You two get to relax and eat while we talk between gulps. I was taught it isn't polite to talk with a mouthful of food. Maybe you'll just have to wait until we're done eating."

"And the dishes are cleared away." Gil winked at his wife.

"And the coffee's made and we're all settled inside around the fire," Claire continued.

"Will you both stop teasing and talk?" Reagan said as she unfolded her napkin. "The suspense is killing me!"

Claire took up the story.

She drove through McDonald's on her way home, grumbling about what a fool she'd been to go to the Holiday Inn, expecting Gil Hunt to actually show up.

She had just finished her fries when the phone rang.

"Claire?" It was Gil, but she acted as though she didn't recognize his voice.

"Yes?"

"This is Gil . . . Gil Hunt? The strangest thing just happened."

He sounded so nonchalant, as though they talked every day.

"What happened?"

"I was walking through the hotel lobby and just felt that there was a message from you. It was this . . . overpowering sensation. Really weird. So I asked at the front desk and they gave me your note."

"You forgot our date?" She tried disguising her embarrassment with a hint of anger.

"No, no, no. Well . . . I remembered the day and place, just not the time." He didn't tell that he'd waited for hours. He had his pride.

"Well, I guess I'll see you tomorrow, then, at the convention."

"Hey, wait. My invitation still stands. For dinner?"

"I already ate," she said, looking down at her greasy hamburger wrapper.

He didn't tell her he'd eaten, too—not during that conversation anyway. "Well, if you'll come back tonight, I'll buy you a drink."

She liked the way he sounded, and it all came back to her: how kind he had been, how charming. "I don't know. . ."

"Come on, Claire, it's early. Not even nine o'clock. Please?"

Ah, begging. That was almost as good as chocolate.

"I'm really tired." She didn't want to give in just yet.

"I'll tell you what," he said. "If you come back, I'll buy you two drinks. And we'll go anywhere you like."

"Two drinks," she replied, bargaining, "and you have to run out to my car when I pull up in front of the hotel." Now she was having fun.

"You've got a deal," he agreed readily.

And that was what he did. He waited in the lobby, shifting impatiently from foot to foot, peering out the front door, his friends—Michael and a couple who wrote mysteries together—watching and waiting to see the woman who had him acting this way. Finally, when she pulled up in her car, he went trotting out, as he'd said he would. She saw people inside, their noses pressed to the glass doors, trying to see her behind the wheel. Later, she thought what good friends he had, how much they loved him, which was further indication of the type of man he was.

He ran around the car and slipped into the passenger seat. She remembered that he smelled good, looked somewhat contrite, and how her heart raced because they'd finally gotten together.

"Where to?" she asked.

"Your choice, remember?" he replied.

Right across the street was another hotel. It had a bar, too, and restaurant called Jodhpurs. She drove there, and the trip was strictly a symbolic one, just to be able to say she had picked him up and they had driven somewhere to talk.

"Only he did most of the talking," Claire told Tucker and Reagan, "just went on and on about what a bad year he'd had, and how he'd looked forward to this."

"In my defense," Gil said, "I was nervous."

"And his body language was . . . well, weird," she said. "We sat at this high table, had drinks, and he kept his body turned toward the door, like he was going to run out at any minute."

"I don't remember that," he said, shaking his head. "I recall I was very happy to be there."

Reagan put her knife and fork down, pushed her plate a few inches away, and said, "So what happened then?"

"We closed the place down." Claire said.

"See?" Gil interjected. "I didn't run out."

"And then we went across the street to a bar in his hotel."

"Spankys," he said. "I remember that."

"And we talked and closed that place down."

"They close early in Omaha."

"And then he took me to his room to see his hot tub," Claire said.

"I did not!" Gil protested. "I mean, I had a hot tub, but I never even thought about it when I asked her to my room. I wanted to show her how nice it was, with a kitchen and a fridge."

"Yeah, yeah," Reagan said, exchanging looks with Claire. "They're all alike, aren't they?"

"And," Claire added, pausing for effect, "he left his pack of condoms out in the bathroom for me to see."

"They happened to be in my toiletry bag."

"Which you left open."

"Why would I close it?" he asked. "I hadn't expected to take anyone up there."

The women exchanged another glance, and Tucker said, "They got you nailed, boy."

"Then his friends started showing up for his annual poker game," Claire said, "and he shoved me out the door with a quick 'Good night.'"

"I never shoved you."

"You didn't even walk me to the elevator."

"Gil!" Reagan said.

"I know, I know," he said sheepishly. "I thought about it too late, after I was trapped behind the poker table, but I apologized later."

"Profusely." Claire smiled.

Reagan leaned in. "You saw each other the next day, right? The courtship continued, right?"

"Well," Gil said, "let's get dessert on the table, and then we'll tell you how the courtship continued . . . with a slight detour for the murder."

CHAPTER 10

FRESH AIR. It hit her the minute she walked out of the joint. *Damn, but it smelled sweeter being outside.*

The ratty gym bag was light in her hand. *Hell, why shouldn't it be?* There was nothing in there except for the Kmart skirt and blouse and those ugly running shoes that everybody'd been so hot for eight years ago. The envelope with the dough the asshole guard had shoved at her as she walked out the gate hardly made a bulge in her back pocket.

They were right about the way prison changed a person. She was eight years changed.

She'd gone into prison unprepared. Sure, she'd been convicted, but she'd had no previous record, no run-ins with the law. And that, she figured, was enough to set her apart from the bitches and whores who deserved to be there. When she went inside, she'd known nothing of the life of a criminal —and that's what they said she was, a criminal.

So she'd had to learn that life—and she had. She'd been lucky enough to find some damn good teachers inside. Some of those teachers hadn't exactly been trying to help her, and some of those lessons she'd learned the hard way. She hadn't been able to escape those eight years without physical pain and scars to show for her time.

The first two years had nearly broken her, fighting off the dykes, the guards, and anyone else who wanted a piece of her. But she'd gotten quicker by year three. Learned not only how to cover her ass but how to bury her emotions, as well.

On year five, she'd died. Her hopes, any plans for a new life outside of the goddamned prison walls, all of it. And out of the grave rose a different animal, baptized with the unholy water of that stinking place.

And after eight years? This was a totally resurrected person, one who bore no resemblance to the spirit that once inhabited that body.

The rusted-out ash can caught her eye and she shit-canned everything. From this moment on, she'd be brand-new.

Stuffing her fists deep in the pockets of her windbreaker, she walked to the road to wait for him.

Before she could begin again completely, she had something to do, a goal to accomplish that would officially put adficio to her former life.

Yes, she had even read some Latin while inside.

Iniuria.

Revenge.

CHAPTER 11

"MURDER?" Reagan said. "You can't just drop a word like that on

us and then go get dessert."

"Actually," Gil said, "it's not something we like to talk about, but, unfortunately, it is part of our story."

Claire carried an apple pie to the table, followed by Tucker, who balanced a tray loaded down with a carafe of coffee, cups, and silverware.

"Claire," Reagan implored, "come on. You're killing me here."

"Um, it's really more Gil's part of the story. He should take it from here."

They started in on dessert and Gil said, "Well, the murder really didn't happen until the end of that next day. . . ."

Back then, there wasn't much to do on Thursday. The convention traditionally started running panels on Friday.

Thursday was a day for early registrations and for people to catch up with friends they hadn't seen for a year.

Gil was having lunch with a group of people, but he managed to be in the lobby when Claire arrived, and he invited her to join them. She accepted immediately.

Lunch was pleasant. Afterward, Gil caught up with some friends, introduced them to Claire. Even that early in their relationship, he felt pride in the fact that she was there with him.

They didn't stay together for the entire day, as each had an agenda. They agreed to meet later for the cocktail party, which would officially open the convention and introduce the guest of honor.

Gil got to the ballroom first because he was anxious to see Claire again. She would tell him later that she didn't want to appear too anxious, so she arrived a few minutes late. It was all part of the game.

Robin Westerly was a man who had been writing critically acclaimed mystery and Western novels for over twenty years. For some reason, however, this was his first turn as guest of honor. Also attending with him was his new wife, Gloria, an aspiring writer. Both husband and wife were in their late forties.

However, Mrs. Westerly was not very well liked by the writing community. Robin Westerly had never been very accessible to fans, and things had only gotten worse since he had married Gloria.

For this reason, when Gil saw Gloria from across the floor, he made no move to approach her. Instead, he spent his time saying hello to other writers he knew, all the while watching the door for Claire.

"Gil!"

He turned and saw Dave Spenser, one of the convention organizers, coming toward him. He and Dave had met many years ago, when both were new to mystery conventions, and since then each had become well known in the field.

"Hello, Spense. Nice turnout."

The two men shook hands.

Spense, a painfully thin, bearded man in his forties, looked around and said, "This is only the half of it . . . I hope."

"Don't worry. It'll be great."

Dave looked over Gil's shoulder. "Have you seen Robin anywhere?"

Gil shook his head. "Nope."

"Well, he and Gloria got here early, but you know how she is. She keeps him from mingling. Very passive-aggressive."

"He's not two years old; he's a grown man. Free to come and go as he pleases."

"I know you're one of the people here who has thought for years that Robin's a horse's ass, but wait till you get a load of him now. He's worse."

"Big egos don't impress me, Spense. You know that," Gil said.

"Whatever," Spense said. "I have bigger problems right now. I'm going to have to go and get him if he doesn't show up soon."

"Well, maybe that's what he wants," Gil said, "for you to go to him."

Spense made a face. "I don't know why I do this to myself. This has got to be the last time I organize one of these things."

"I've heard that before."

"And what's this I hear about you having a new woman in your life?"

"What?"

"It's going around."

"Well, that's not exactly right, but there is someone here —and there she is."

Claire had just entered the room and was looking around—he hoped—for him.

"Very nice," Spense said.

"Not your type. Too old—she's not sixteen."

"Bite me," Spense said. "Introduce me?"

"Maybe later. I'm still getting to know her myself. Besides, if you'd been at the poker game last night like you promised, you would have met her."

"She was in your room?"

"Briefly."

"Fine," Spense said. "Don't share. I've got my own problems anyway."

"Catch you later."

They went their separate ways, Dave to wait for his guest of honor, and Gil to talk to his.

CHAPTER 12

GIL BOUGHT Claire a drink at the cash bar, told her how nice she looked, didn't tell her how much he'd been looking forward to seeing her again that night.

"What's this guest of honor like?" she asked him, nervously making conversation.

"Well, right now," Gil said, looking at his watch, "he's very late."

From across the room, Gil could see Spense fidgeting, anxiously watching the door. He wondered idly if that was how he had looked to people while waiting for Claire to show up.

Suddenly, Spense was coming across the floor toward him.

"Gil, I—"

"Claire, this is Dave Spenser," Gil said, cutting his friend off. "Dave is one of the convention organizers."

"Nice to meet you," Claire said.

"Yes, nice to meet you, too. Gil, would you do me a favor?"

"What's that?"

"Go to Westerly's room and see what's holding him up?"

"Why me?"

"Because I can't leave here, his wife refuses to go and find him, and because you know him."

"Dave—" Gil said, sliding his eyes Claire's way, hoping his friend would catch on.

Instead, it was Claire who caught on. "Come on," she said, "I'll go with you."

"Really?"

"Sure. I'd like to meet the illustrious Robin Westerly."

On the way to the elevator, Gil filled Claire in.

"So everyone thinks his new wife has changed him?" she asked. "That doesn't seem fair."

"Well, Robin was never easy to talk to, and he wasn't a regular attendee at these cons, but since he hooked up with *her,* they come all the time. This is his first appearance as guest of honor, and as I understand it, she lobbied for him to get it."

"She sounds like a real go-getter."

"That's one way of putting it," Gil said.

"So, what do you think of her?"

"Well," he said as they reached the elevator court, "I've always had the feeling she thought once they were married, she'd get a book deal."

"You think she married him just to get published? Isn't that a little coldhearted?"

Before he could answer, the elevator doors opened and a group of conventiongoers got out. When they spotted Gil, they stopped and asked what he was doing. After he told them about his errand, they all decided to tag along.

"What's the point of going to the cocktail party if the star isn't there?" a man asked.

"Hey, the more the merrier," Gil joked. "Maybe when he sees a mob outside his door, he'll move a little faster."

So they all piled into the elevator. Gil and Claire's conversation had to be put on hold for the time being.

got off on the fifth floor; they were a rowdy crowd by now. Claire looked amused as Gil led the way along the corridor to Robin Westerly's room.

As they arrived at the number Dave Spenser had given Gil, he noticed the door was ajar.

"What's wrong?" Claire asked when he didn't knock.

"It's open."

Claire took charge, immediately turning and telling the others— five or six men and women—to settle down.

"What's going on?" someone asked.

"Something's not right," Claire said.

Gil wondered if he should call security, but he didn't want to look like a wuss in front of Claire. So he knocked and then entered.

"Hey! Robin!"

Immediately, he saw the body on the floor. There was so much blood that he didn't notice the maid. When he did look up, he was surprised to see the woman standing there. A woman who appeared to be in shock.

"Jesus. Someone call the police! Hurry. Call nine one one."

"Who is that?" a man asked, trying to get a closer look. He only succeeded in pushing Gil, causing him to bump into the frightened maid.

"Who are you?" Gil asked her.

She suddenly came to life. Looking at Gil with a panicky expression, she moved slowly at first and then bolted from the room. The crowd was pushing through the door, clogging the hallway. None of them stopped her.

Finally, someone started for the phone, but Gil said, "No! Find a house phone. Don't touch anything in this room. In fact, everybody out!"

He turned to Claire, found her frozen with fear.

"Is—is he dead?" she asked.

"I don't know, Claire," he said, taking her by the shoulders. "Let's go outside and wait for the police."

She walked stiffly as he ushered her to the door and told the gawkers to leave.

"Hey, this is something, huh?" one of them said. "Just like *Murder, She Wrote.*"

As Gil closed the door behind him, he thought this was nothing like a TV show. The man on the floor would never be getting up, and he certainly would never be making another guest appearance.

CHAPTER 13

"MY GOD," Tucker said. "I had no idea you two were involved in anything like that."

They had all finished dessert and the table was now a graveyard for their dinner—plates, glasses, utensils, half-empty coffee cups.

Gil found the look Tucker was giving him to be somewhat accusatory. "There's never really been a reason to bring this up before," he explained.

"When someone asks how you two met, do you always include the murder?" Reagan asked.

"No," Claire said. "We usually edit that part out. But we're among friends here. Besides, celebrating our anniversary—all the memories, excitement—we got carried away, I guess."

Reagan reached out and grabbed Gil's hand and then Claire's. "Hey, we care about you both. Tucker told me you didn't want your story in my book, and I promise—cross my heart—that I will respect your wishes. Everything we say here tonight will forever stay among just the four of us."

Claire squeezed Reagan's hand. "You know we wish

you nothing but success with your book, Reagan." She glanced at Gil, who was nodding in agreement. "It's just that we're afraid it might seem as if we're trying to profit from someone's death. Besides, it's all so tragic, and your book should be upbeat."

Reagan smiled and sat back. "I fully agree. But that doesn't mean you can't tell us what happened, right?"

Tucker agreed.

"Why don't we get this table cleared away first?" Claire suggested. Gil stood up and rubbed his hands together. "It's getting chilly out here. I suggest we move inside."

"And we have a little anniversary gift for the two of you," Tucker said. "I'll be right back."

"It's in the car," Reagan explained. "A selfish gift, really. You'll have to share it with us."

By working together, the women cleared the table in record time. Tucker had returned with a very expensive bottle of champagne, and after popping the cork, he helped Gil build a fire inside the cozy cabin.

"This is so nice," Claire said as she settled into the over-stuffed chair in front of the fire. Reagan sat on a corner of the matching sofa and held out her arms for Tucker to come join her. Gil poured champagne and passed the glasses around.

"To the most interesting people we know," Tucker said, raising his glass.

Claire laughed. "Ditto."

"Yeah," said Gil, "the archaeologist and the artist. Not your average couple."

"And a bookstore owner and TV shopping hostess are normal?" Tucker asked.

"Okay, so we all agree the four of us are unique, wonderful, and charming," Reagan said. "Now how about getting back to your story?"

"I think it would be better if Gil told the rest of it straight through."

Reagan and Tucker exchanged a look and he said, "Suits us."

"I just want to find out what happened," Reagan said. "The suspense is still killing me."

Gil sat on the arm of Claire's chair. "Well," he said, "let's see how I can best tell this. . . ."

CHAPTER 14

THE DETECTIVE in charge of the Robin Westerly murder was a man named Ed Donovan; however, he didn't arrive until after two uniformed officers responded to a frantic call made from the hotel. Before the police were called, the hotel manager and head of security had both been summoned. But Gil refused to allow them to enter the room.

"Are you a police officer, sir?" the nervous manager asked.

"No, but we've all seen enough *Law and Order* to know that you don't contaminate a crime scene. We have to wait for the police." Gil stood firm.

"How do you even know this is a crime scene?" the security man asked.

"There's a man lying dead inside that room," Gil told them. "What would you call it?"

"How do you know he's dead?" the security man shot back. "Did you check him? Maybe he's hurt and we're wasting time standing out here arguing."

"He was shot in the head. . . ."

The security man listened to Gil with his mouth hanging open, then said, "But he could still be alive. I've seen *Law and Order,* too, and I know it can happen."

Gil was on shaky ground here. After all, he had not checked the body, so how could he be certain Westerly was dead?

"If I get our house doctor down here, will you let him in?" the security man asked.

"Why the hell do we need his permission to enter?" the manager demanded. "There's two of us and one of him."

"There's more than one of him," Claire said, taking hold of Gil's arm.

"Yeah," some of the other conventioneers chimed in. Thank goodness, Gil thought, that I asked them not to leave until the police arrived.

"If you get your doctor down here," Gil said, "he can go in and confirm that Mr. Westerly is dead."

The security man looked at the manager. "That's fair."

The manager tossed his hands in the air.

By the time the doctor came out of the room, two uniformed officers were exiting the elevator.

"What's going on?" one of them demanded. "Why are you all blocking the hall?"

"We're all waiting for you," Gil said, and explained about the body inside the room. He also introduced the doctor.

"Well, Doc, is there a dead man in that room?" the taller of the two asked.

"There certainly is," the physician replied. "He's been shot through the head."

"What is the approximate time of death?" Gil asked. He

was hoping that his taking control of the scene had not been foolish.

"That'll be up to the ME," the man said. "I can only tell you that he was, in fact, shot and is dead." He looked at the police. "May I leave now?"

"I'm sorry, Doc," the shorter cop said, "but you'll have to wait until the detective arrives." He turned to the people in the hall. "You'll all have to wait, too."

"That's what *he* said," the manager responded morosely, pointing to Gil.

"And you are?" the tall officer asked.

"Gil Hunt. I found the body."

"We all found the body!" someone shouted, not wanting to be left out. Gil was somewhat appalled that the mood among the conventiongoers had remained festive. Maybe that would change when the enormity of the situation hit them.

"Gil was the first," Claire said.

"And you, ma'am?"

"Claire Duncan. I was right behind him."

The cop turned to his partner, who was writing in a small notebook. "Get everyone's name and I'll call it in."

"Right."

The next to arrive was Ed Donovan and his partner, Jerry Lyle.

After viewing the body, the first thing Donovan did was to ask the manager if there was an empty room on that floor.

"Well, we're quite full. . . ."

"Sir, I need a place to question all these people. That is, unless you'd like us to keep this hallway roped off all night— or, better yet, we could use the main lobby."

"No, no, we can't do that," the manager said, rubbing his sweaty hands along the seams of his suit pants. "I'll check and see. I'm sure we have a room available on this floor."

Not only did they have a room but it turned out to be a two-bedroom suite.

"Excellent," Donovan said when he saw it. "Jerry, get me one of the first cops on the scene."

"Sure, Ed."

Lyle returned with the taller cop, whose name was Hal Jenkins.

"Officer, who discovered the body?"

"Fella named Hunt. Claims he entered the room ahead of his group, Detective."

"'Claims'?"

"There were a lot of people with him," Jenkins explained, "but he was apparently the first one in. He also took charge and safeguarded the scene."

"Sounds like a smart man," the detective said. "Bring him in here. I'll start with him."

"Yes, sir."

"As for the others, my partner will start taking statements in the other part of the suite. Have your partner—"

"Sam Pezullo, sir."

"Yes . . . have Officer Pezullo begin bringing them over there."

"Yes, sir."

Jenkins ushered Gil into the room for his first meeting with Detective Donovan.

CHAPTER 15

"ED DONOVAN."

"Gil Hunt."

"Glad to meet you," Donovan said, extending his hand, "just not under these circumstances."

"I know what you mean."

"Have a seat."

Donovan walked across the room and closed the connecting door to the other part of the suite. Gil was surprised that such a large man with hands as big as footballs would close the door so gently, then walk softly to a chair and settle himself into it so very gracefully.

"Mr. Hunt, why don't you fill me in on who the victim was, who you are, and why you were both here."

"What do you want to know, exactly?"

"Just keep talking," Donovan said. "If I have any pressing questions, I'll interrupt, but what I'd like is just for you to tell me everything you can think of. Keep talking until you have nothing left to say. By that time, if I don't have everything I need, I'll definitely ask some questions."

And so Gil started to talk. He told Donovan about the

convention first: who was attending it, how often the con was held and why. Then he spoke about himself, and his business. Finally, he told the detective what he knew about Robin Westerly, both the man's career and what little information he had about his private life.

True to his word, the detective sat quietly and listened, never interrupting once until Gil was finally done.

"Well, that was very comprehensive. Are you a writer yourself?"

"No, I just sell books."

"I have a few more questions, if you're up to them."

"Sure, go ahead."

"You seem fairly calm for a man who discovered a dead body."

"I'm waiting until I'm alone to dissolve into tears," Gil said. He knew the remark sounded like something straight out of a Richard Stark novel, because he'd read hard-boiled fiction for years, but it wasn't too far from the truth.

"I'll try not to keep you much longer, then," Donovan said.

"That's all right," Gil said, trying to make up for the remark. "I want to help."

"And we appreciate it. In fact, you've helped quite a bit already. You knew enough to safeguard the crime scene. Must be all those mystery novels you read, huh?"

"It just seemed to make sense."

"So, tell me, who makes sense for this?"

"Excuse me?"

"Who do you see for this crime?" Donovan asked. "You know this crowd. You knew the victim, who his friends were—"

"Detective Donovan," Gil said, "this is an annual event. Most of these people see one another once, maybe twice a year. That doesn't give them—me—any insight into some-one's private life."

"None of these people ever see each other privately?" the detective asked. "As friends?"

"I'm sure some do, but—"

"What about Westerly? Was he close to any of these other writers?"

"He wasn't a particularly friendly or warm man."

"I'm sorry, but I've never heard of him," Donovan said. "Was he famous?"

"Well, no. . . . He was respected in the field, but certainly not a bestselling author."

"Not like, uh, Stephen King? Or . . ." Donovan was stuck for the name of another famous writer, exposing his ignorance of such things.

"No," Gil said, "not like Stephen King."

"Mickey Spillane!" Donovan said proudly.

"Right, nothing like Mickey Spillane."

"But he made his living this way, right?"

"Yes."

"And would anyone benefit from his death?"

"Personally, I couldn't say," Gil replied. "You'd have to talk to his wife about that."

Donovan closed his eyes for a moment, then opened them and said, "Gloria, right?"

"Yes."

"And professionally?"

"I just can't see how anyone would profit."

"Was he in someone's way?"

"What do you mean?" Gil asked, frowning.

"Well, will someone move up now that he's dead? Take his spot with his publisher? Do you have—I don't know—ranks?"

"It's not that kind of business, Detective. But, as I told you before, I'm a bookseller. You'll probably have to talk to his agent, or publisher—"

"Can you give me some names?"

"I can tell you who his publishing company is," Gil said, "but you'd have to get his agent's name from his wife, and his editor's name from her also."

"So there are a whole lot of questions you can't answer."

"Tons."

Donovan hesitated a moment, seemed to be collecting his thoughts. "All right," he said finally, "tell me about the people who were with you."

"Conventiongoers," Gil said. "They were in the elevator, heard where we were going, and decided to tag along."

"'We'?"

"Excuse me?"

"You said they heard where '*we* were going,'" Donovan said. "That means that at least one other person was already with you when you got into the elevator. Who was it?"

Gil hesitated. He didn't want to get Claire in trouble, but she was going to be questioned no matter what.

"That would be Claire Duncan."

"And she is?"

"An attendee . . ."

"And a friend of yours?"

"We . . . we met here, in Omaha, at this convention a couple of years ago. This year we're . . . just getting to know each other better."

"Ah," Donovan said, "a budding romance?"

"No," Gil replied, embarrassed. "It's nothing like that."

"But things like that do happen at conventions, right?"

"I suppose."

"Just a few more questions, Mr. Hunt, and I'll let you go. Is this considered one of the larger conventions?"

"It's a regional one. The big mystery convention—called Bouchercon—moves from state to state and takes place in the fall. There're usually anywhere between fifteen hundred to two thousand people attending. But this one is much smaller and is only a few years old."

"With how many in attendance?"

"About three or four hundred, I'd imagine," Gil said. "You'd have to speak with one of the organizers to get exact numbers."

"So, we have three or four hundred suspects."

"More, I'd think."

"Oh? Why more?"

"Well," Gil said, "I'm no policeman, Detective Donovan, but who says the killer has to be attending the convention?"

Donovan stared at Gil for a few moments, then said, "Very good point, Mr. Hunt."

CHAPTER 16

BEFORE LEAVING, Gil said, "There's one more thing."

"What's that?"

"When we entered the room, there was a maid inside."

"What was she doing?"

"Just . . . standing there."

"Had she touched anything?"

"I don't know."

Donovan stretched out his long legs. "Well, Mr. Hunt, you seem to have pretty good instincts. What do you think she was doing? Did you happen to catch a name? Was she wearing a name tag? Any kind of ID?"

"I don't know the answers to any of those questions," Gil said. "I remember thinking that she looked as if she was in shock, and when I tried to speak to her, she bolted from the room."

"And nobody stopped her?"

"Listen, Detective, I know this is all routine for you, but it's not for me or for any of the rest of us. After I saw Westerly, everything else sort of blurred for a minute. Besides, the woman moved quickly. I can't speak for the others, but the first thing on my mind was not tackling a stranger."

"I understand," Donovan said. "Just give me a description, then."

Gil did, trying to be as thorough as possible.

"I assume you're staying in this hotel?"

"Yes, sir."

"I'll need your room number."

Gil gave it to him, and then the detective walked him to the door. When he opened it, Gil saw one of the uniformed officers standing outside with Claire.

"Gil?" she said.

"It's okay."

"Is this the lady who was with you?" Donovan asked.

"Yes. Detective Donovan, this is Claire Duncan."

"My pleasure, ma'am. Would you mind coming inside so I can ask you a few questions?"

"Sure," she said.

"Thank you for being so helpful," Donovan said. "It makes my job a little easier."

Claire looked at Gil, who touched her arm and said, "I'll be waiting out here."

She told him later that the way he'd said that, and touched her, meant a lot. She also told him what had transpired inside.

Claire sat in the chair Gil had just vacated, and Donovan reclaimed his.

"I'm sure this has been very upsetting for you, Miss Duncan."

"Mrs."

"I'm sorry, Mrs. Duncan. Mr. Hunt filled me in on the

convention and who's who. Would you just tell me why you're here?"

Briefly, Claire told the detective her story, why she had attended the convention for the past two years and had come this year. She did not tell him that she was interested in Gil romantically.

"So you didn't know the victim?"

"I haven't even read any of his books."

"Are you an avid reader?"

"Oh yes," she said, "but I've only started reading mysteries recently."

Donovan smiled. "I don't have much time to read for pleasure, but when I do, I usually stick to biographies. I've never heard of Robin Westerly."

"I've heard of him. He's a big shot around here."

"Do you know any of his history?"

"No."

"Do you know his wife?"

Claire shook her head. "Never met her or heard of her."

"Then I guess all you need to tell me now is what you saw when you entered the room."

Again, Claire described things as briefly as she could, telling him what she had seen. It annoyed her that her voice shook when she spoke.

"What can you tell me about the maid?"

Claire told him everything she could remember, which wasn't much.

"To tell you the truth, Detective," she said, "I found it difficult to take my eyes off the body."

"Is Westerly's the first you've seen that was a product of violence?"

"You mean my first murder? Yes."

"I'm sorry," he said. "I can certainly understand how you wouldn't have been aware of much else."

"I only wish I could be more help."

"Maybe you can."

"How?"

"Tell me what you know about Gil Hunt."

"Not much," she said. She had no way of knowing what Gil had already said, and she didn't want to say anything that would get him into trouble. Then again, what was there for her to say? The truth was, she really didn't know him that well, so that's what she said.

"You're not a couple?" Donovan asked.

She gave the detective's left hand a quick look and saw he was wearing a wedding band.

"No," she said. "Why? Did he say something to that effect?"

"No, not at all." The detective stood up and buttoned his jacket. "Well, I think I have all I need from you, Mrs. Duncan—except your address."

"I live here in town. I'm in the book."

"Excellent."

She stood and he walked her to the door.

Outside in the hall, Gil waited impatiently. He watched as the others were ushered through a door and into the other part of the suite.

The manager and doctor were gone, but Gil noticed that the head of security was sticking around. He sidled over and stood beside the man.

"Guess you have to stay to represent the hotel?"

"No. I'm waiting to be questioned."

Gil stuck out his hand. "Gil Hunt, by the way."

The man looked at the hand for a moment with basset hound eyes, then gave Gil's hand a limp shake.

"Steve Kerr."

"This is my first murder. Has this ever happened to you before?"

"Twelve years in this business, I've seen a lot of dead bodies, but this is my first murder." The man looked at Gil. "You showed a lot of balls, keeping us out. Where are you from?"

"New York."

"Hmm," Kerr said, facing front again. "Maybe that explains it."

Gil had the feeling he'd just been insulted.

CHAPTER 17

WHEN DETECTIVE DONOVAN opened the door to let her leave, Claire saw Gil waiting for her and got a funny feeling in the pit of her stomach. She told him years later that it was just one of the many loving gestures he'd made so effortlessly—tiny things he was hardly aware of, but monumental compared to the disregard she had experienced throughout her life.

In the time it had taken Donovan to interview Gil and Claire, his partner had interviewed and cut loose the rest of the witnesses. The only one left to be interviewed was Steve Kerr.

Claire stepped into the hall and Gil came forward and placed a protective hand on the small of her back.

"Okay?" he asked.

"I'm fine."

Donovan looked from one to the other, then said, "We'll be in touch if we need anything else. I'm sure neither of you will be leaving town for a while."

"No," she said, then looked at Gil.

"Not until the convention is over," he said, then added, "That is, if it still goes on."

"Yes, well," Donovan said, "if it gets canceled, I'm afraid everyone will need permission to leave—but we'll cross that bridge when we come to it. I still have to talk to the organizers, who, no doubt, have heard the news by now."

Gil realized the man was right. By now, the news had probably filtered down to everyone at the convention—-up to and including the victim's wife.

"We pulled her aside and told her privately," Donovan replied when Gil put the question to him. "She's been in her room all this time."

"That was very sensitive of you, Detective," Claire said.

"Thank you, Mrs. Duncan."

Gil could see the detective had been charmed by Claire, and he was surprised to feel a twinge of jealousy.

"Mr. Kerr," Donovan said as his partner came up behind him, "we're ready for you now."

Kerr nodded and moved past Gil and Claire.

"Good luck," Gil said.

"Thanks."

Donovan gave the couple a brief smile and then closed the door.

"Whew!" Claire said. "I'm so glad that's over."

"You've handled this whole thing pretty well," Gil told her. "I'm impressed.

"Me?" she asked. "What about the way you took charge? That was very brave."

"Okay," Gil said, "now that we're both suitably impressed, maybe a drink is in order."

"Only one?" she said. "I think I need some time to let everything that's happened here sink in."

They decided to take the time in the hotel bar.

However, drinking alone, especially under the bizarre circumstances, was impossible. Not only had word of Westerly's death gotten around but also the fact that it had been Gil Hunt who had found the body. As soon as they entered the crowded bar, they were besieged with questions, most of which were coming from Dave Spenser, who grabbed Gil and pulled him over to the side.

"What the hell is happening?" he hissed.

"Somebody killed him, Spense," Gil said. "That's all I can tell you.

"Killed him how?"

"Shot him."

"Jesus!" Dave covered his face with both hands. "This is terrible!"

"It sure is."

"What am I supposed to do?" Dave asked. "He was the guest of honor."

"Oh, you mean that kind of terrible."

"No, no," Dave said, "don't get me wrong, Gil. It's awful that he's dead, but what do I do now with four hundred people? Cancel?"

"I wouldn't advise it."

"Why not?"

"The detective in charge told me he doesn't want anyone from the convention to leave town yet. If hundreds of people are going to be stuck here, they need something to do."

"That makes sense," Dave said, "but how does he expect to keep everyone here? I mean, some of them live in town and aren't staying at the hotel."

"He's going to ask you for a complete list of attendees. Do you have it computerized?"

"Of course," Dave said, "everyone who puts on a convention does that."

"Then if I were you, I'd get busy printing out lists."

"Lists?"

"Yes," Gil said, "try a list of fans, a list of writers, and break it down by location. Give him a separate list of those who registered here at the hotel and those who are locals."

"That's a good idea," Dave said, calming down somewhat. "Keep the con going, print out lists."

"And pick a replacement guest of honor."

"Oh, right, right, gotta do that . . . but who?"

"Who's here?" Gil asked.

"Larry Block? Al Collins? I'm going to need someone who can step in at a moment's notice and be good," Dave said, half to himself.

"Well, good luck," Gil said, patting him on the shoulder. "I've got to get going. There's a lady waiting for me."

"Yeah—hey, thanks, buddy. You gave me some good advice."

"No problem."

Gil returned to where Claire was still trying to field a barrage of questions. He pulled her aside.

"What's happening?" she asked.

"We can't talk here. Let's go someplace else and have that drink."

"Food, too?" she asked. "I know just the place."

CHAPTER 18

CLAIR TOOK Gil to her favorite Mexican restaurant. It was just down the street a few blocks, on Dodge. Well after the usual dinner hour, a table was easy to come by.

"What time do they close?" Gil asked as they were seated.

"You still have about an hour," the hostess told him.

A waiter came over and took their orders immediately. They asked him to bring the drinks—a beer for him and margarita for her—right away. When they had their glasses, she brought hers up to her nose and inhaled deeply.

"I love margaritas," she said, "the salt along the rim of the glass, especially the glass. It feels good in my hands." She took a sip. "God, I really need this tonight. I've never seen . . . what I saw today . . . before."

"Neither have I."

"What are they going to do now?" she asked.

"Who? The cops or the convention people?"

"The conventioneers, I guess."

The waiter returned with a large basket of chips and a stoneware bowl of salsa. Claire nibbled on a chip while Gil told her about his conversation with Dave Spenser, and the advice he had given him.

"Wow," she said. "That was good thinking. Detective Donovan will be so pleased."

"So will Spense," Gil said. "He would have had a heart attack if he'd had to cancel. Now all he's got to do is find a replacement guest of honor."

"I still can't believe it," Claire said, wiping her hands and straightening up. "Here we are, talking about . . . I've never seen . . . blood, like that."

He reached across the table and took her hand. "I'm so sorry I subjected you to that."

She squeezed his hand. "Don't be so noble. How were you to know what we'd find? And remember, I wanted to go with you."

"Well," he said, "if I'd reacted a little more quickly, I might have been able to keep you from seeing . . . him."

Their orders were ready, and as the waiter arranged plates, each let go of the other's hand and sat back.

"This looks good," Gil said.

"I feel terrible that I can eat," she said, "but I'm so hungry, it hurts. I get that way when I'm upset. Nothing stops my appetite."

Gil cut into his enchilada. "Me, too."

"So, what are you planning to do now?" she asked between bites.

"Uh, well, I guess I'll attend the convention, like I planned. Sell some books."

"You think people will be in a buying mood?" she asked. "Want to attend panels? Do the usual stuff?"

"People are resilient," Gil said. "And curious."

"And, unfortunately, bloodthirsty," Claire said, shaking her head.

"Unfortunately, yes. But most will be trying to make sense of it, theorizing. You've got to admit that they'll be talking about it for years to come. The mystery convention where a mystery writer was murdered."

"You're right," she said. "It does make it sound exciting —in a macabre sort of way."

"I'll have to be at my table tomorrow," he said. "I have some Robin Westerly books with me."

"You won't raise the price, will you?" she asked, staring across the table at him.

He knew some of the dealers would do that, especially if the books were signed. "I don't think so," he said. "That would just be . . . ghoulish."

"I agree," she said, secretly glad he had said that.

After dinner, she drove him back to the hotel and they sat in her car for a few moments.

"So, you'll be in the dealers' room tomorrow?"

"Assuming it's open," he said, "and right now I'm operating on that premise. What are your plans?"

"Well, I'm registered," she said. "There are some authors I'd like to see and a few panels that sound interesting."

Suddenly, he was nervous. "Okay, then. Good. I'll see you tomorrow."

"I guess you will."

"Maybe we can have lunch," he said, "or dinner."

"Won't you be busy at your table?"

"I can get somebody to cover for me," he said, "or I can just shut down for a while."

"If you do that, you'll lose money."

He shrugged. "It's only money."

She smiled. "You're so sweet. Well . . . I'll see you tomorrow, then."

"Right," he said, "tomorrow."

There was an awkward moment and then he suddenly leaned over and kissed her—that is, he meant to kiss her. What he actually ended up doing was grazing her cheek with his lips. Then he got out of the car and stood there feeling like a dope as she drove away.

"Lame-o," he said to himself, and went into the hotel.

CHAPTER 19

WHEN CLAIRE GOT HOME, she immediately made herself a cup of tea and sat down on the sofa, pulling the chenille blanket over her. She couldn't stop shaking. Never before had she experienced anything like she had that day. It was odd, frightening, and under normal circumstances she would never return to that hotel again. But Gil made the difference. She had felt a connection with him that she had never felt before, not even with her ex-husband. Stronger than her fear was the desire to know Gil Hunt better. The possibility of something wonderful developing between the two of them could only happen if she went back there, to the place where she'd seen something horrible.

When she closed her eyes, she could still see the blood, and the paleness of Westerly's head. The smell of him, of death, seemed to have followed her home.

She needed a long hot bath. Taking her cup with her, she headed for the bathroom. A box of scented bath beads was on the vanity and she dumped a few into the steaming water as it filled up the tub. Some candles might also help, she thought. Anything to dispel the odor that lingered in her nostrils.

But what, if anything, could dispel the visions in her head?

When Gil entered the hotel, he thought about going to one of the bars, but they'd both be filled with conventioneers, and the thought of spending the rest of the evening fending off questions about Robin Westerly sickened him. He decided to go to his room instead.

When he got there, he found a note taped to his door. "No game tonight?" it said. It wasn't signed. He pulled the paper down and crumpled it in his hand. People were more resilient than even he, with his inborn New York cynicism, had imagined. Somebody— maybe more than one some-body—had expected that there would still be a poker game, even after a murder had been committed.

He entered his room and tossed the note in the waste-basket. Then he fell down across the bed and rehashed the events of the day, still unable to make sense of it all.

He'd started out very anxious to see Claire again, and get to know her better. He'd never met a woman before whom he was so eager to know. It could have been a perfect day spent with her except for . . .

He rubbed his hands over his face, and suddenly the shakes started. It took a while for them to run their course, and he remained on the bed until they had. When his insides finally stopped quivering, he got up, went to the refrigerator, and took out a bottle of beer. He gulped half of it, then set the bottle down on the countertop, gasping. It was then he noticed the round table in the corner, still set up with cards, chips piled in the center.

Poker. He usually looked forward to playing when he came to this convention. It had become a lifeline for him since his divorce, this game with his friends, but now it didn't seem important at all. One minute, one tragedy, and so many things changed. Now spending time with this wonderful woman who had come into his life seemed more important than playing poker.

Did he feel so upset because he had been the one to find Robin's body? he wondered What if he were just like most of the other convention attendees and had only heard about the murder—not actually seen the victim up close? Would he then be concerned just with the convention continuing, only half-caring about who the new guest of honor was? Or would he be concerned with the poker game going on as scheduled? Or simply trying to make sure now that Claire was in his life, she would never leave?

Or would this murder, the violence, the horrible scene he had walked in on, forever change the way he viewed everything from now on?

He wondered if Detective Donovan would be able to solve the mystery before the weekend was out. Maybe that would go a long way toward wiping it from his mind.

Maybe.

CHAPTER 20

GIL HAD breakfast in the hotel dining room, and, as he'd feared would happen, many people were eager to join him. He put them off by saying he just wanted to enjoy his meal and forget all about the murder. Apparently, many of them would have been thrilled finding a body and then talking about it, because they looked at him as if he were crazy—but at least they left him alone.

He was down to his last cup of coffee when Dave Spenser walked in, spotted him, and came walking over.

"I'm almost finished and I don't want to talk about it," Gil said, in hopes of heading him off.

"Neither do I," Dave said, sitting down. "I need a favor."

"Okay."

"You're friends with John Barry Williams, right?"

Williams was a successful writer of hard-boiled novels and was on a slightly higher plane than Robin Westerly had been.

"Why?"

"I want him to step in as guest of honor."

"He's not here, Dave," Gil said.

"But he lives in St. Louis. He could be here in no time, if you called him."

"Dave, John wouldn't do it," Gil said. "You'll have to find somebody else—somebody who's already here."

Dave averted his eyes.

"Wait a minute," Gil said. "You've already asked?"

Dave nodded. "Five people. They all said no, for one reason or another." He looked at Gil. "Do you think they're superstitious?"

"What do you mean? There's some ancient law about being a guest of honor at a mystery convention?" Gil tried not to laugh.

"No. Maybe they don't want to step in for a man who was murdered. Maybe they think there's some deranged serial killer who'll finger them next."

Gil opened his mouth to say that was ridiculous, then closed it again as he reconsidered. Then he said, "Naw, I don't think so. They probably just came here to have a good time, like the rest of us, and don't want to take on the responsibility."

"All they'd have to do is make a speech at the banquet."

"Which is tomorrow night, right?"

"Right."

"Then you have the better part of two days to keep asking," Gil said. "Try Parnell Hall. He'd probably love it. Or what about Jerry Healy?"

Dave snapped his fingers and said, "Two good ideas. Got any more?"

"Ask them first. If they say no, I'll suggest a few others."

"Thanks. You're a big help, Gil."

"Well, I try."

Dave grabbed a piece of toast Gil had left on his plate. "So, have the police been around today?" he asked.

"I haven't seen them, but I'm sure they'll show up. Did they talk to you last night?"

"Yeah, but I couldn't tell them much. I didn't know Westerly that well."

"What about his wife?"

"I don't know her, either, but from what I hear, she's a real bitch. I think the cops talked to her in her room last night. She hasn't been down yet today. I wonder if she'll ever come down . . . although . . ."

"Although what?"

"Well . . . some of our less forgiving friends think she may be burning up the phone lines trying to generate some publicity out of this."

"For her husband's novel?" Westerly had a new book coming out, which was supposed to debut at the convention.

"Or her future ones."

"Ah."

"Well," Dave said, licking a smudge of jelly from his finger, "I got things to do. You gonna be doing some business in the dealers' room today?"

"For a while."

"Until the lady shows up?"

"Who knows. . . ."

"You're not the type for convention romances, Gil. At least you never have been before."

"And I'm still not," Gil said. "This is no convention romance."

"Okay," Dave said, standing. "'Nuff said, then. I'll see you later."

"Yeah," Gil said, looking for the waiter, "later."

Gil was in the dealers' room, doing business, when Claire walked in. He felt his heart make a leap, and a trapdoor in his stomach opened, releasing a rush of butterflies.

He didn't wave, having decided to wait until she came over to him. He had his pride.

CHAPTER 21

CLAIRE KNEW Gil had seen her as soon as she walked in. As part of the game, she decided to stroll around the dealers' room, pretending to examine some of the books at the other tables before going over to him. The game was important to her. Too many people in her life were running on anger and regret; too many had forgotten the little pleasures life offers up for the creative. And she really enjoyed the fact that Gil would play along.

She had awakened that morning after a restless sleep filled with nightmares. But the bad dreams had just seemed to fuel her determination to return to the convention and see Gil. Something had gotten started between them, and she meant to see it through. A comforting aura surrounded Gil Hunt. She had felt it immediately, back at their first meeting, two years before. And as she flipped through pages of books she didn't even focus on, she could feel her heart racing, but she forced her legs to move slowly.

Gil saw Claire circling the room and smiled to himself. It

had been a long time since he'd met a woman he wanted to play with. His wife and he had never been playful together. What had kept him in that marriage for so long? he often wondered.

He was mulling that over, keeping his eyes on Claire, when he noticed someone else enter the dealers' room. The man wasn't wearing a convention badge, but Gil knew he had another kind of badge in his pocket. It was Detective Donovan.

The detective stopped just inside the door and looked around the room. Unlike many of the dealers' rooms Gil had been in at past conventions, this one was spacious, with a high ceiling and plenty of elbowroom. He was used to bumping into people, both behind the table as well as in front of it. For this reason, it was easy for the detective to spot the person he was looking for—who, apparently, was Gil.

Instead of taking the circuitous route that Claire had chosen, Detective Donovan walked directly to Gil's table. For this reason, he beat Claire there by several tables. Gil saw her stop short as Donovan reached him.

"Good afternoon, Mr. Hunt."

"Detective," Gil said. "I don't suppose you're here to buy some books?"

"Oh, I don't know," Donovan said, scanning the titles displayed on Gil's table. "Have you got anything interesting? Like a Raymond Chandler?"

Gil wondered if the man was trying to show off some odd bit of knowledge he had stashed inside his brain or if he was a reader.

"I've got a Chandler first edition here," Gil said. He took down a copy of *The Big Sleep,* coated with Mylar to protect it, and handed it to the detective. The price was written on a sticker, and when the man saw it, he whistled and gingerly handed the book back.

"That's not a book," he said; "that's a down payment on a car."

"What did you have in mind, then?"

"Oh, I don't know," Donovan said, "How about a Robin Westerly?"

"You're in luck," Gil said. "You can get that from just about any dealer in the room."

"I see," Donovan said. "Then he's not particularly, uh, collectible?"

"No more or less than any other contemporary author," Gil said. "Why?"

"I was just wondering about motive."

"Do you think someone killed him to make his books more valuable?"

"It works with painters, doesn't it?"

"I suppose it does."

"But you don't buy it, huh?"

"Not in this case, no."

"Then maybe you can take some time to talk to me about a few things?"

"Like what?" Gil asked.

"Like the things you told me yesterday. I just need some insight into this business, and these people."

Gil looked confused. "But why me?"

"You found the body," Donovan said, "so you're already involved. And you seem intelligent."

"Gee, thanks," Gil said sarcastically, all the while watching Claire, who was standing at the next table, turning a book over in her hands.

Donovan followed Gil's eyes. "Am I interrupting something?"

"You might be."

"You can ask the lady to join us for coffee," Donovan said, "or lunch."

Gil looked at him. "Are you interested in her, too?"

"Only insofar as she's attending the convention," Donovan said. "And she was with you when you found Westerly."

Claire instinctively knew the two men were talking about her, so she boldly walked over.

"Hello, Gil."

"Claire, you remember Detective Donovan, don't you?"

"Of course. How are you, Detective?"

"Fine, Mrs. Duncan, but I'd be better if you could talk your friend here into having lunch with me—and inviting you along, as well."

"Me?" she asked. "Why would you want to have lunch with me?"

"I have some questions for the two of you," Donovan said, "and I get the feeling you would have been spending time together today anyway. Besides, two heads are better than one. The more details you can remember, the more efficiently I can do my job."

"Now it sounds like you want to grill us. I thought you just had a few questions to ask over coffee," Gil said.

"Well . . . lunch would be better, give us more time. What do you say?" He looked at Gil and then to Claire. "The city will pay."

Gil and Claire exchanged a glance and had a moment of total understanding. They had no way of knowing then that it would be the first of many such moments they would share throughout their years together.

"All right," Gil said, confident that he was speaking for both of them, "lunch it is."

CHAPTER 22

GIL GOT someone at the next table to cover for him and then went to lunch with Claire and Detective Donovan.

"You trust folks like that?" the detective asked on the way to the hotel restaurant.

"The dealers watch out for one another," Gil said. "If there's any stealing going on, it's usually after hours."

"How do you prevent that?"

"A good lock on the doors helps," Gil said. "Also some extra attention from security, if the convention can get it."

"That Chandler book you showed me, you leave that in the room overnight?" Donovan asked.

"Not if I can help it."

Claire stood next to Gil when they reached the restaurant. The place was filling up for lunch, but they were able to get a table fairly quickly.

Gil ordered a burger, Claire went for the Cobb salad, Detective Donovan ordered a grilled cheese sandwich, and they all had coffee.

"You want fries with that?" the waiter asked Gil.

"No."

"How about you?" he asked Donovan.

"None for me, either, thanks."

As the waiter walked away, Donovan patted his stomach and said, "Guys our age have to start watching our weight and cholesterol—all those numbers."

Gil was embarrassed that Donovan was making him feel old in front of Claire. "I just didn't want to take too long," he said. "Got to get back to the table. Can we start your lunchtime investigation, Detective?"

"Sure, of course," Donovan said. "I'm still trying to get a handle on the people involved here."

"How do you know who's involved?" Claire asked.

"I just mean the . . . mystery-writing people. Authors, editors, publishers . . . book dealers," Donovan said, pointing to Gil.

"What do you want to know?" Gil asked.

"I talked to this fella . . ." Donovan took out his note-book and consulted it. Gil had the feeling he didn't really have to, that he was just doing it for effect. "Dave Spenser."

"What about him?"

"He seems . . . nervous."

"I'll bet he does."

"Why's that?"

"He's the organizer of this whole thing," Gil said. "If it's a flop, it's on his head."

"Does he lose money if it flops?"

"I'm not sure how these things work," Gil said. "I don't know if he's on the hook financially. . . . You'll have to ask him what the arrangements are."

"Is he usually a nervous guy?"

"He can be."

"You mean just because he comes across as being nervous, which he probably is because of this whole murder investigation, you take it to mean he's hiding something?" Claire asked, a bit perturbed.

"I thought it was a possibility."

"Dave was hosting a party in the ballroom when Westerly was killed," Gil said.

"And you know that because you were there also?"

"That's right."

"So, by giving him an alibi, you're also giving yourself one."

"I'm not giving him an alibi," Gil said, "or myself. Talk to anyone who was there; they'll say they saw us."

"And you were there, in the ballroom, until he asked you to find Westerly."

"That's right."

Donovan paused a moment to collect his thoughts, then said, "Well, all right."

"Have you talked to his wife yet?" Claire asked.

"Yes, this morning. She seemed . . . bereaved."

"'Seemed'?"

"Yeah. I don't know, but it didn't feel right. It was almost as if she was acting the part of the sad widow from one of her husband's novels." Donovan shrugged. "Just giving the old detective what he wanted."

Claire looked at Gil, as if asking for confirmation that this was what Gloria Westerly was like. He could only raise his eyebrows.

"I don't know the woman that well," Gil said. "You'll have to ask someone who does."

"And who would that be, Mr. Hunt?"

"I don't know."

At that point, the waiter came with lunch, set out plates in front of the threesome, and left.

"Well," Donovan said, "I guess I'll leave you nice people

to your lunch." He picked up his sandwich and wrapped it in a napkin, then stood up. "Don't worry, I'll take care of the check. Thanks for your help, both of you."

Gil and Claire watched as Donovan walked over to the waiter, passed him some money, and then left the restaurant. Then they looked at each other.

"What help?" Claire wondered aloud. "The man didn't ask me one question. Do you think he was being sarcastic or just very sneaky about something? Trying to trip us up. You know, more can be said with silence than by volumes of words. Why did he even want me here? Gil? What do you think?"

Gil didn't know what he thought about any of it. Deciding to take the easy way out, he pointed toward her salad. "That looks good."

CHAPTER 23

"OH, I forgot to ask the detective something," Claire said halfway through lunch.

"What?"

"About the maid. I was wondering if he'd been able to find her and interview her."

"Good question," Gil said, "but the poor thing was so frightened of what she'd found that she might still be running."

When they finished lunch, they waited while the waiter cleared the table and refilled their coffee cups. Gil decided that since he finally had Claire to himself, he'd take the opportunity to get to know her better. He had no intention of rushing back to the dealers' room. "This is kind of odd, isn't it?" he said.

"'Odd'? You mean having lunch with a detective? Walking into a murder scene?"

"I mean us, meeting under these circumstances," he said, "connecting the way we have—we have connected, haven't we? I mean, I'm not fooling myself, am I?"

She thought about teasing him, then decided this was

not the time to play, since he was being so sincere. "No, you're not wrong. We've definitely connected."

"I hate to sound . . . callous," Gil went on, "but it seems like this whole . . . murder investigation has been thrown in our way."

She raised her eyebrows. "I don't believe it. I was thinking the same thing. Isn't that so . . . egotistical of us?"

"Maybe it is," Gil agreed, "but it's how I feel. I just wish they'd all go away and give us some time to get to know each other."

She looked at her watch. "Speaking of time, don't you have to get back?"

"The hell with it," he said, putting his elbows on the table and his chin in his hands. "I want to talk about you."

She mimicked his pose and said with a smile, "Only if you talk about yourself, too."

So they stole a few moments that afternoon to learn more about each other before the investigation really got in the way.

Several cups of coffee later, they were still engrossed in conversation, but not so much so that they didn't notice the person who had entered the restaurant.

"Is that who I think it is?" Claire asked.

"Yes," Gil said, "that's Gloria Westerly."

"The artificially grieving widow, according to Detective Donovan."

"How did you recognize her?" Gil asked.

"She was pointed out to me at the party last night, before we left. Who is she with?"

One of the waiters showed Gloria to a table, along with the two other women in her group.

"I know one of them," Gil said, "the tall one is Sasha Peters."

"The Chicago author?" Claire asked. "The one who writes about the lady PI?"

"That's her."

"She's a bestselling author, isn't she?"

"Is that what they say?"

Claire looked a little disappointed. "You mean she isn't?"

"She's made some of the extended lists," Gil said, "but she's never made the top ten."

"Still . . ."

"Yes," Gil agreed, "still."

"I wonder what she's doing with Gloria Westerly."

"Maybe they met through Robin. I really don't know, but somewhere along the way they became friends."

The three women were given menus and then the waiter left them to make their decisions. As Gil and Claire watched, the three women began to laugh.

"It sure seems like Donovan was right," Gil said. "She doesn't look very bereaved."

Claire turned around in her chair. "Maybe her friends are cheering her up."

"If your husband had been killed less than twenty-four hours ago, could you be cheered up?"

"Well—and we're talking about my ex-husband here—yes. In fact"—she rubbed the place on her left hand where her wedding band had been—"I'd also be doing a dance of joy."

"Good point," Gil said, remembering his own harsh feelings toward his ex-wife. "But maybe you'd be doing your dance in private—just because that's the kind of classy broad you are."

She laughed. "You really are starting to know me. So, why don't you go over and talk to her?"

"Me? What for?"

"Aren't you curious?"

"About what?"

"About her, and her husband," Claire said. "Just go over and see how she reacts when you give her your condolences. After all, you are the one who found him. She should have something to say to you."

"Like what?" he asked.

"'Thank you'?"

CHAPTER 24

GIL HAD to admit that he was curious about how Gloria Westerly would react to him. Before he stood up, he wiped his face with the napkin that had been folded in his lap. "Do I look okay?" he asked Claire.

"Fine." She patted his arm. "Now get over there, so you can hurry back and tell me everything."

"Here I go." He stood up, pushed his chair in, and walked over toward Gloria and her companions. As he approached, they stopped talking and all three looked up at him.

"Can we help you?" Sasha Peters asked.

She was older than the two women she was with. Gray hair and a handsome, if somewhat lined, face gave away her seniority.

"My name is Gil Hunt."

"Oh, yes," Sasha said, "you have a table in the dealers' room, don't you? Old Delmar Bookstore in St. Louis, right?"

"That's right."

"Oh, my God," said the woman who was unfamiliar to him. Her hand quickly went to her mouth, as if she were trying to hold the words back. "You found—" She stopped and looked at Gloria.

"Yes," Robin Westerly's widow said, "you found my husband's body."

"Sorry to say I did," Gil said solemnly. "I wanted to offer you my condolences."

"Thank you. And I suppose I should thank you for finding him."

"That's not necessary."

She dropped her hands into her lap and shrugged. She had large eyes, very blue, and he was surprised how clear the whites were. Crying generally made one's eyes red.

"I'm just sorry it happened. . . . I hope the police haven't been too . . . rough on you."

"Detective Donovan, you mean?" she asked, casually checking out the manicured nails on her right hand. "No, he's been doing his job. I've been moved to another room because the one we were in is now a . . . a crime scene."

The third woman reached out to touch her friend's arm, but when Gloria didn't respond, the woman removed her hand quickly.

"I think he suspects me," Gloria said.

"What?" Sasha looked horrified. "Why, that's silly. Don't you think that's ridiculous, Mr. Hunt?"

"I think it's standard procedure for the police to start a murder investigation with the spouse, Mrs. Peters. But she was in the ballroom with hundreds of people at the time, so I don't think he seriously suspects her."

"Maybe not," the third woman said, "but it must be horrible to think you're suspected of your own husband's—"

"Murder," said Gloria, finishing her friend's statement. "You can say the word, Angela. Robin was murdered by someone at this convention."

"But . . . but who would do such a thing?" Angela asked. Gil recognized her now. Her name was Angela Beldon and she published a fanzine featuring book reviews and author interviews.

"Somebody who was jealous of him, I guess," Gloria said.

Before he could stop himself, Gil asked, "Jealous of what?"

"His success, of course," she said, "his talent, and, most of all, his position in the mystery community."

Gil frowned but held his tongue this time, even though he thought Mrs. Westerly had an exaggerated opinion of her husband's reputation in the "mystery community."

"Well," he said, unsure of what to do next, "I didn't mean to interrupt your lunch. I just wanted to tell you how very . . . sorry I was."

"Thank you again, Mr. Hunt," Gloria Westerly said. "I truly appreciate that." Looking up at Gil, she gently touched her hand to her heart. "And I know Robin would have appreciated your kindness also. He often told me how important fans like you were to his career."

"Ladies," he said, hoping the word didn't sound as angry as he suddenly felt. And then he retreated to his table before he said something he'd regret.

"I wonder what he wanted?" Sasha Peters said, watching Gil walk away.

"He seemed pretty straightforward to me," Angela said. "He came over to say he was sorry."

"Do you know how he happened to find Robin?" Sasha asked Gloria.

"Not exactly," Gloria said. "I only know that he did."

Sasha reached out and touched Gloria's arm. The gesture did not escape Angela's notice, and she felt hurt seeing how much more willing Gloria was to accommodate Sasha.

"You poor thing . . ." Sasha cooed.

Before Gil even had a chance to sit down, Claire asked excitedly, "So? What happened?"

"Not much," he said, scooting his chair closer to the table. "She doesn't seem very upset, and she certainly is under the misconception that her husband was more important—or more popular—than he was."

"What did you say?" Claire demanded. "And what did she say?"

"Word for word?"

"Of course!"

Gil found himself repeating the conversation, Claire hanging on his every word.

"And her eyes weren't red?" Claire asked when he had finished.

"Nope."

"Do you think that means she hasn't been crying?"

"Looks that way to me."

"They do have drops, you know—to take out the redness."

"I suppose she could have used something like that," Gil said.

"Maybe you should call Donovan."

"Why?" Gil asked. "I haven't found out anything he doesn't already know. He seems very thorough. I wouldn't want to waste his time, or embarrass myself."

"I suppose."

Gil checked his watch.

"You have to get back to your table?"

"Only if I want to make a living."

She smiled. "I'll go with you ... if that's all right?"

He smiled back. "It's very all right."

CHAPTER 25

"YOU'RE GOOD AT THIS," Gil said as Claire wrote up a sale.

"Comes from lots of experience in all kinds of jobs. I figure by now I'm qualified to do practically anything."

Gil bagged the books for his customer and thanked him. After straightening a section of the table, he sat down again. His chair was touching Claire's, and he liked the cramped space. "For instance?" he asked.

"What?"

"Give me a list of the jobs you've had. I bet my list is longer than yours."

"How much?"

"Dinner," he said.

"Is that all? How about something bigger?" she joked. "A lady of my breeding requires much chocolate and junk jewelry."

"Okay, if you win, we'll go to the nearest Target and you can shop till you drop. But if I win, you have to take me to the nearest mall and let me spend some money on you."

She was really starting to adore this man. He was not

only funny and charming but so easy to be with, it was unsettling at times. Her ex-husband used to say that her independent nature was her biggest flaw. He used to complain that she didn't need anyone. Unfortunately in his case, it was true. But Claire had always thought of herself as self-sufficient, and considered it a good thing, what women were supposed to strive to be. She also knew that if she let him, Gil would become a vital part of her life—a life she was now somewhat fearful to share.

"Okay, my first job was in Chicago. I was seventeen and worked in the toy department at Marshall Field. The next summer, there was a job, also downtown, and I was a proofreader. Then came six months at Time Books, then buyer for a department store, a finance company, Western Union, another department store, a greeting card store, a radio station, the music store a friend was opening and needed help with, and then—finally—my journalism degree kicked in and I started getting jobs at small TV stations."

"How many of those?" Gil asked, looking amazed.

"About five."

"Well." He added up the numbers he had been writing on a scrap of paper. "According to my figures, you've had about fifteen jobs."

"Sounds right."

"And I know for a fact that I've only had six. So you win. Hands down, you're the most—"

"Gil Hunt!"

The couple looked up, to see a well-dressed white-haired man smiling the most photogenic smile Claire had ever seen. The word that immediately came to her mind as she studied him was *dashing*.

"Les!" Gil raced around to the front of the table and embraced the man. "God, you look wonderful."

"You're looking well yourself," Les said, and then broke away to extend a hand to Claire. "And who's this pretty lady?"

Claire stood and shook hands. "Claire Duncan."

"Claire, this is Les Roberts," Gil said.

If Les had been wearing a hat, he would have tipped it at Claire, but instead he gave a slight nod. Then turning toward his friend, he confided, "Everybody's whispering about this new lady in your life, and now I see what all the commotion is about."

Gil's cheeks were warming, but he hoped no one would notice. "Claire, Les is the most charming man you'll ever meet, but he's also one of the most . . . popular? Is that how you'd put it, Les?"

Les smiled even wider. "I like women. So sue me. I'm an all-American red-blooded man."

"And also the author of the Milan Jacovich series."

Claire nodded. "I'm familiar with the books," she said. "In fact, about two months ago, I read *Pepper Pike*."

Les looked flattered. "Take good care of this one," he said to Gil. And then to Claire, he said, "I like you."

It was Claire's turn to blush.

"Well, guys, I got a meeting with my agent and then a panel, but maybe we can have a drink later?"

"Sounds good," Gil said.

"It'll give me a chance to find out all the gory details about Westerly. You know," he said thoughtfully, "sometimes karma does bite you in the ass, doesn't it? Robin was one person I definitely will not miss. But you"—he hugged Gil again—"I wish we could get together more often, old friend."

"Me, too, Les," Gil said.

Claire was struck by the true affection the men shared for each other.

Gil watched Les walk away.

"How long have you been friends?" Claire asked.

"Oh, years. Did you know his books outsell everyone's—King's, Koontz's, Clancy's—in Cleveland. He's a god there."

Before Claire could comment, a couple carrying large book bags stopped in front of the table. "You can run, but you cannot hide from us," the woman said.

"Gil Hunt, long time no see," the man said.

"John," Gil said excitedly, "where have you been hiding?"

"Barb and I just got in this morning."

Gil pulled Claire closer to the couple. "Claire, these are two of my dearest friends, John and Barbara Lutz."

Claire smiled and shook hands. "Are you the John Lutz who's responsible for *Single White Female*?"

John rolled his eyes, "That's the Hollywood name. The book is called *SWF Seeks Same*."

Barbara pointed proudly, "We got to do a scene in the movie. I'm so excited."

"Not really a scene, just a walk-on," John said, trying to downplay the whole thing, but it was obvious he was happy about it. "The cast was great, though; they each made a point of talking to us."

Barbara was a few inches shorter than Claire. While John explained more details of the movie shoot to Gil, she slipped her arm around Claire's waist and whispered in her ear, "It's so good to see Gil happy. He's been through a lot of bad stuff lately."

Claire instantly felt a special bond with the personable woman. "I think we're good for each other," Claire said.

"How about the four of us having dinner tonight?"

Barbara asked. "We need more time to talk about everything. And by everything, I mean the whole Westerly mess."

Gil looked at Claire. "Our first double date—what do you think?"

"I think we can handle it." Claire laughed.

"Good," John said, "we'll meet you back here when the dealers' room closes. It'll give us time to decide where to go."

"Great," Gil said.

When they were alone again, Claire told Gil how much she liked his friends. "You're very lucky to have so many people in your life who obviously care about your welfare."

"I know. But I hope they're not getting too carried away and scaring you."

"Don't worry, the only person scaring me today is that guy."

Gil stretched to look in the direction Claire was pointing. "Oh, that's Wendell; he works here."

"In the dealers' room?" Claire asked.

"No, in the hotel. I've known him for three years now. He's a nice guy."

Claire tried not being too obvious, but she couldn't keep from looking at the huge man. He could have passed for one of those hokey wrestlers on TV. He was bald and big and . . . scary.

"Well, he's been staring at you all day," she said. "I even saw him watching you while you were talking to Mrs. Westerly at lunch. But I guess since he works in the hotel—exactly what is his job?"

"Doorman, bellhop, driver, concierge—he does it all. Last year when he heard I wanted to go to the track, he drove me over there on his lunch hour."

"That was nice of him."

"Wait, you'll see; I'll introduce you." Gil waved to the man lurking in the corner. When Wendell did not respond to Gil's overture, Claire felt even more uneasy.

Gil stood up and waved with both hands.

Realizing Gil had seen him, Wendell rushed out of the room.

"Huh," Gil said as he sat down. "That was weird."

"Why don't you go ask him what's wrong?"

"Maybe he didn't see me," Gil said. "Maybe he was just staring—you know, thinking, not really looking at us."

"Go after him and make him tell you why he's been . . . stalking you," Claire insisted.

"Okay, if it'll make you feel better."

"It will. And if you're not back in ten minutes, I'll send out the hounds."

CHAPTER 26

"WENDELL!" Gil shouted as he chased after the man. "Wait up!" But Wendell kept walking—down the hallway, through the lobby, and out a side entrance of the hotel. Gil ran to catch the doors before they slammed shut. They were heavy glass, coated with a gold reflective paint to keep the sun out. As Gil moved forward to open the door, it was being pushed from the other side. He struggled for a moment, then backed up a step and waited.

"Gil, you're just the person I'm looking for," Dave Spenser said as he burst through the door. "Some coincidence, huh?"

"Hold on a minute, Spense," Gil said as he rushed outside. Looking from one end of the parking lot to the other, Gil scanned the length of the building. The sun was bright and he had a difficult time seeing far. But no matter what the conditions, it was quite clear that Wendell was nowhere in the vicinity.

Giving up, Gil walked back into the hotel, where he found Spense standing exactly where he had left him.

"What was that all about?" Spense asked.

Gil was still distracted, trying to figure out what was happening. "Nothing . . . I just thought . . . Never mind. You said you were looking for me?"

"Yeah, can we go someplace private? To talk? I need to bounce something off you."

Gil thought about Claire waiting for him. "Now's not really a good time. I've got the table—after lunch is always a busy time. Can it wait until later?"

Dave's face fell. "I suppose. . . . It's just that I really need to ask you something."

"Can't you ask me now? Here?" Gil was tiring of Dave's vagueness.

"No, I'd feel better outside the hotel."

"But someone's waiting for me."

"Claire?" Dave asked.

"Yeah, I can't just leave her alone. . . ."

"Gil, I'm begging you, as a friend. I need some help. Please." Dave seemed almost afraid, and it was that look on his face, that pained confusion, that persuaded Gil to hear him out.

"All right, all right. Hold on a minute. I'll be right back."

When Gil entered the dealers' room, he found Claire having an intense conversation with another woman about the latest Grafton novel. The two seemed to be having such a good time, he almost felt guilty interrupting. But after dazzling her with his smile and promising to fill her in on every little detail later, she agreed to man the table. And when she told him to take his time, he wondered where had she been all his life.

The place outside the hotel turned out to be a Village Inn a few blocks away. Each of them ordered coffee and a slice of pie.

"All right, Spense, you got my attention, so now tell me what's wrong."

"That detective came to see me this morning."

"After questioning you last night?"

Dave nodded, looking glum. "Yup."

"You have an alibi; you were with all of us for opening ceremonies. There're hundreds of people who can vouch for you."

"That's what I told him."

"I don't understand, then," Gil said, confused.

"Money. He must have asked me twenty questions—all about money."

"Give me a for instance," Gil said between sips of coffee.

Dave mimicked Donovan: "'So, Mr. Spenser, is there a lot of money to be made from a convention like this? Do organizers do it for the money? Does a famous guest of honor bring in more money?' On and on like that. What do you think I should do, Gil?"

Their pie had arrived, and while Gil listened, he ate.

"Come on, pal, I need some advice here," Spense grumbled.

"I don't understand why you think you have to do something. The detective questioned you, and you answered every question with an honest answer . . . didn't you?"

"Of course." Spense looked indignant.

"There are committees and reports that you have to oversee, right?"

Spense nodded.

"I don't know what kind of money we're talking about here—I've never run a convention—but I don't imagine it's enough to kill for. And if Donovan is going on the assumption that Robin Westerly brought people in, why would you kill your main attraction?"

"Publicity. Television coverage. Since Westerly was killed the first day out, maybe Donovan suspects that the murder was planned to bring crowds, curious types who would never normally attend a mystery convention, especially not with 'our kind of people.' Can you believe that's what he called us?"

"You mean mystery fans?" Gil asked

"Yes. To hear him talk, we're all bloodthirsty, murdering thrill seekers."

Gil couldn't stop laughing. When he finally caught his breath, he said, "You have got to be kidding. I've spoken to Donovan several times, and he never acted like that. Maybe a little unfamiliar with the whole concept of the event but never contemptuous of anyone."

"So, he spoke to you several times? Did you wonder why? Everyone else got a few minutes of questioning."

"I found the body. I would expect to be of more interest to them."

Spense thought a moment. "I guess you're right."

"Relax, Spense. A terrible thing happened and the police are just trying to do their job. The more we all cooperate, the sooner things will get back to normal."

"But I'm worried that with all the questions and inconvenience, people will leave early. There's a lot at stake here, Gil. I've been working on this convention for two years. Everything has to go right."

"So, Donovan's questions were hitting too close to home, then? You do stand to lose money here?"

"Some. But mostly my reputation. I can't have my name

ruined like it was—" Spense stopped abruptly, hoping Gil hadn't noticed.

But he had. "Like it was when? I don't remember anything happening."

"Oh a few years ago, there was this rumor going around, that's all. It wasn't anything. Forget it."

"A rumor about what?" Gil asked.

"There was this place I used to work at—a computer place. They had some trouble with their auditors. It was all a misunderstanding. Nothing to it." Spense shoved the rest of his pie into his mouth.

At that moment, Gil realized how little he knew of Spense's real life. He knew he lived in Seattle, had been divorced twice, had no children, and was a terrible poker player. And that was about it. Despite calling this man his friend, he'd seen him only once or twice a year for the past ten years.

Gil checked his watch. "We better get back. Hope I helped."

"I guess I'm just stressed-out. It's been real crazy. Lots of writers equal lots of egos. Keeping everyone happy gets challenging at times."

"I bet." Gil grabbed the check that had been left on the table. "I got this one."

"Thanks," Spense said. "I owe you."

CHAPTER 27

REALIZING HE MISSED CLAIRE, Gil smiled. Seeing her sitting there behind his table, surrounded by so many of his friends, reinforced his feelings that she fit perfectly into his life. He slowed down his pace as he approached, watching her reading one of the newer paperbacks. All too quickly, his contentment turned to unease. What if she didn't think he fit into her life? A book dealer. It sounded so . . . so . . . boring. He hadn't had time to tell her how much he traveled, all the interesting people that inhabited his life. And for the first time since he'd discovered poor Robin Westerly, he asked himself if he was enjoying the extra attention from his colleagues and Donovan? Did it make him feel important in front of Claire? Then she looked up from her book and saw him. Her face brightened and their eyes locked. His fears drifted off to another part of his brain.

"You walk like a dancer," she said.

"Where did that come from?" he asked, startled but flattered.

"I was noticing the way you move. I like it."

He couldn't speak right away. She made him feel self-conscious.

"So?" she asked. "Did Wendell tell you why he was skulking around like that?"

"Never spoke to him," Gil explained. "I spent all this time with Spense."

"Wow." She shook her head. "I think I missed something here."

"Come up to my room—no funny business, promise. You can freshen up before dinner and I'll explain everything."

"Sure, but what about your books? Isn't it too early to close up shop?"

"I have an in with the boss." Gil winked. "Come on."

Graciella Sanchez was a real beauty—when she wanted to be. At work, she went without makeup and wore her hair pulled back tightly. She could almost fade into the background. People never recalled meeting her until being introduced for the third or fourth time. But when she wanted to be remembered, she was an expert at making a lasting impression. Her shiny black hair, olive complexion, and small frame made her appear almost regal. With those huge eyes, the long lashes, she could be carrying on a conversation and make her companion abruptly stop and say, "You're really a beautiful woman, you know that?" She'd look down demurely, shake her head, but she knew. And while the uniform she was forced to wear at her job in the Holiday Inn was drab and practical, her casual wardrobe consisted of tight-fitting, bright, sexy clothes.

"Just talk to him. Gil Hunt's one of the good guys."

"No! Jesus, Wendell, stop telling me what to do! Just because we live together, you have no right to tell me what to do with my life!"

Wendell walked up behind her. At six two, he stood more than a head taller. He tried putting his arms around her, but she shoved him back with her elbows. "No! Get away from me!"

"Gracie, baby, stop. You didn't do anything, so why are you running away? Think how it'll look if the cops don't find you here."

She furiously continued to throw clothes into her suitcase. "So they got my address from personnel—big deal. When they come here, asking a shitload of questions, you tell them I went home to visit my sick mama. Tell them what a good daughter I am, sending my paycheck to my poor relatives in my tiny village. They'll eat it up."

"This isn't some damn cop show on TV, Gracie; it's real life! Our life!"

She spun around. "Oh no, don't you do that. We are not married. I am not your wife. This is my life. My bad luck to be in that shitty room at the wrong time. Got it? My problem."

"No, *you* don't get it. This is our problem—we're in this together."

"You have no idea what can happen. I've seen it. I've lived through it with Lupe."

"Yeah, yeah, I know all about your sister. But, baby, she was running drugs."

"No! Hector was, not Lupe! Not my sister." When she suddenly broke down crying, he held her.

"This is different. This isn't Mexico."

"You'll never get it, will you?" she said. "I'm a woman."

"Try being a black man."

"What the hell does that have to do with anything?" she shouted, breaking free of him. "This is your country . . . your home. You understand the language—all the little jokes everyone laughs at—you know the customs, the people. No matter what I do, I'm the foreigner. If something is missing from one of the rooms I clean, they question me. If the room isn't cleaned to everyone's satisfaction, it's because I'm lazy. I can never do anything right."

He'd finally had enough and threw her suitcase across the room. "There are people out there who are gonna come down hard on you, no matter what you do. Nuthin' is ever good enough. Nuthin' is ever their own damn fault. But you can't let 'em call the shots, baby. Gracie, trust me. I'm not gonna let anything bad happen to you." He held out his arms to her. "You're right; it is your life. But I love you and I'm just tryin' to keep you from fuckin' it up."

CHAPTER 28

BY SATURDAY, the Holiday Inn was overflowing with fans, visiting authors, booksellers, agents, anyone associated with publishing mystery novels. Either Robin Westerly's murder had had no effect on the crowd or it had enticed locals to come on down and mingle with the mystery lovers.

Gil had ordered breakfast from room service and was enjoying his bacon when he was interrupted by an insistent knock. Hoping Claire had decided to start her day early, he hurried to the door. But his spirits dipped when he saw who was on the other side.

"Why do I get the impression that I'm not the person you were expecting?" Detective Donovan asked.

"Oh, Detective, sorry, it's just that . . ."

"No need to explain. I'm used to it by now. Sometimes I think I'm one step below a dentist on the popularity scale."

Gil held the door open. "Why don't you come in? I think there's enough coffee, maybe some juice."

Donovan walked into the large room. "No thanks. But you keep eating."

If he hadn't been so hungry, Gil would have protested,

but he sat back down at the small table. "At least sit down," he told Donovan, pointing across the room to a chair by the desk. "Drag that over and tell me why you're here."

"Still interviewing people, doing the legwork, filing reports—standard stuff."

"I don't think I can tell you anything else, Detective," Gil said, buttering his toast.

"Oh, no, Mr. Hunt." Donovan loosened his tie and then sat down. "I've come for a favor. A big one, and you can say no, but it would sure help me out."

"What is it?"

"This whole situation is a bit . . . out of the ordinary, shall we say:

"That's an understatement."

"And I've never been involved in a murder scene in the middle of a convention."

"That's a good thing. Right?"

"Definitely."

"Okay then, ask away," Gil said. "What's the favor?"

"I'd like you to be my guide, so to speak. I need you to fill me in on who's who, what their jobs entail, how they felt about Mr. Westerly. Give me your take on them. I need gossip, truth, anything that will help me better understand their relationship to the victim."

Gil paused for a moment to think over what Donovan had just proposed. "How many people are we talking about?"

"Oh, six, tops. It shouldn't take that long."

"But I'm here to work, Detective. This is how I make my living—selling books."

"I know, and I apologize. Don't you have someone who can fill in for you?"

"Maybe. I'll have to make a call. Oh, and finish getting dressed."

"Thank you, Mr. Hunt, I really appreciate this." Donovan waited a beat and then asked, "So when do you think you'll know something for sure?"

"An hour."

"Great."

"One question first," Gil said. "Are you so sure I'm innocent that you don't think I might steer you in the wrong direction?"

"To be honest, Mr. Hunt, you and Mrs. Duncan would have to be two of the stupidest people I've come across if you'd kill someone and then go out and leisurely gather up a crowd to accompany you back to the murder scene. If you'd killed Westerly, your first instinct would be to run, unless, of course, you're a cold-blooded killer. Which you are not. Or if you stood to benefit from his murder. Which it seems you do not. No, your reactions were appropriate. Your responses were truthful. And believe me, I've asked around. You are one of the most well-liked, respected men here."

Gil had always been leery of flattery. And he couldn't help but wonder if the detective was just conning him now in hopes of tripping him up. Or was he truly sincere. But the thing that seemed to be controlling his actions over the past few days was the constant dialogue looping over and over through his brain: What if that had been me sprawled out on the floor for everyone to gawk at? Would anyone have helped me? Would anyone have cared enough to spend their time working with the police? Or, instead, would they have spent their time talking about the crime from a bar stool?

So he called Claire, did some begging, and then while

Donovan watched the baseball scores on ESPN, Gil ducked in the bathroom with an armful of clean clothes.

The same room that had been used that first night of questioning had been cleaned, and stocked with bottled water and sodas. From the look of the place, it was obvious the police had set up camp and planned to be there awhile.

The two men waited for the first person—a writer with ten novels under his belt—to show up. The only sound in the room was coming from children running out in the hallway. When he felt comfortable enough, Gil asked, "So, have you questioned the bellman yet?"

"Which one?"

"Wendell. I don't know his last name."

Donovan checked the notepad laid out in front of him. "Ah, yes, Wendell Payne. Why?"

"Oh, nothing, it's just that I've known him for a few years now. He's a great guy. Very outgoing, always offering to go the extra mile. He's filled the refrigerator in my room with drinks before a poker game, driven me out to the track. We've had some good conversations about his job here."

"But?"

"Nothing. I really haven't seen much of him this trip. Well, Claire saw him yesterday—in the dealers' room, standing in a corner. . . ."

"And?" Donovan asked patiently.

Gil wished he hadn't started this whole thing, but since he had, he figured he'd better get on with it. "Claire said she noticed Wendell sort of stalking me. She said every time she looked up, there he was."

"What did he want?"

"That's the strange part. When I tried to ask him what was going on, he took off."

"And you said this was yesterday?"

"Yes."

"And you haven't seen him since?"

"No."

"Did you know that Mr. Payne lives with a woman?"

"No. We never talked about personal things like that."

"Well, according to the manager, it's a relatively new arrangement."

"And why would his living situation be any business of mine?" Gil asked.

"Because the woman he lives with is a maid at this hotel."

Suddenly, Gil got it. "The maid who was in Westerly's room?"

"The very one."

"And you've questioned her?"

"No. It's taken until today to track her down. The hotel recently switched over to a new computer system, so their personnel records were difficult to access. You add that to the fact that there are fifty-two maids on the payroll, you'll see we've had our hands full. There was also a problem finding out just which maid we were looking for."

"You had to wait to see who didn't show up for work?"

Donovan nodded. "Process of elimination. But my men are on it. In fact, two of them are on their way to Mr. Payne's apartment as we speak."

CHAPTER 29

CLAIRE NEVER DID WELL in the morning, but as she sat behind Gil's table, she got caught up in the excitement and enthusiasm of the fans who crowded the large dealers' room.

"Do you have the latest Max Allan Collins? From his Nate Heller series?" asked a teen wearing black jeans, a black T-shirt, and black tennis shoes.

"I think I saw it right there." Claire pointed to a far corner of the table.

"He's great, isn't he? There's always so much research in his books, and they take place in Chicago. Elliott Ness, Al Capone, Frank Nitti—great stuff!"

"Sorry, I've just started reading mysteries and haven't gotten to him yet."

"Oh. Well, when you get time, try him." The kid couldn't stand still as Claire counted out his change. "This is my first mystery convention. I came all the way from Lincoln just to get Mr. Collins to sign my books. I have five of 'em in here." He held up a book bag.

"Well, I hope you have a good time."

"Thanks." And he was off.

Business was steady, but the majority of people who stopped by the table asked for Gil. They wanted to know about the murder.

"I heard he got shot in the arm," said a woman wearing a vest covered with pins from other conventions she'd attended across the country. "He walked in on the killer and had to wrestle the gun away."

"No," Claire said, "he's fine."

"He's working with the police, then?" her friend asked. "Everyone's saying he works undercover . . . part-time."

"How exciting," the vest lady said.

As they chattered between themselves, Claire wondered what she should tell these people. Then she decided to play it safe and say as little as possible. Besides, if word got around that she had some juicy details, a line would form in front of the table and she would become the star attraction.

People continued to stop at the table and more questions flew in her direction. Each time, Claire shrugged and said, "Sorry, I just work here." After a while, the curious got tired and drifted off to talk to other dealers. She hoped she hadn't cost Gil any sales.

The pace began to pick up as the morning wore on. A camera crew set up in a far corner, doing interviews with some of the more famous authors. Convention volunteers walked the room to make sure everyone was happy. Several more volunteers were set up by the two entrances, checking that every attendee had a badge, proving they had paid for the right to be there. Aisles were getting crowded and the noise level in the room was rising.

Several tables down from her, a dealer was selling ornate bookmarks, pens, and jewelry. There were tables piled high with magazines—current and back issues—along-side old pulps and shiny new bestsellers. As she sat there, Claire mentally planned which tables she would visit when Gil returned.

Fifteen minutes went by, then another. Claire had only had time for a quick cup of tea after Gil's call for help. Now she was hungry and had to find a rest room. After asking the dealer at the next table to cover for her, Claire hurried out of the room.

The ladies' room closest to the dealers' room had a line of irritated women backed up to the door. Claire rushed back into the hallway and down to the gift shop, where she remembered having seen rest rooms in the corner next to a bank of pay phones. Her effort was rewarded when she pushed the door open and found she practically had the place to herself. An attractive woman was standing in front of the mirror, fixing her lipstick, and never even glanced up when Claire entered the last stall.

The bathroom was so still, and the Muzak version of one of her favorite songs made her appreciate the first calm moment she'd had all day. But the mood was interrupted by the sound of metal screeching across the tiled floor. After listening for a second, Claire figured out it was a bucket.

"I tell you, LaVonne, he's better off without her."

"That's what I've been tellin' you for months, Ty. He was fine before she come along."

"He's a man of quality, not meant to go slummin' with the likes of that one."

The other woman laughed. "You still carrying on because he didn't want to go out with you, huh? I thought things was better between you two since you embarrassed yourself like that."

"Things was. No matter, though. With her always there, always bitchin' at him, he's different. It ain't the same, no matter what he says."

"Wendell is truly a unique man. Any woman here would snatch that brother up."

Claire's ears perked up at the mention of Wendell's name.

"He swears she ain't like that, though, LaVonne."

"Tell it to my sister. She's got the locker next to that bitch. One day, she notices Gracie has a gun in her locker. One of those big ones, not some little play toy. So she says, 'What you planning to do with that?' and Gracie takes it out, holds it to my little sister's head, and says if she asks any more questions, she'll find out."

"But LaVonne, I still don't understand why she'd go and kill that man? Don't you find that bizarre even for her?"

"Graciella comes from money. She's used to nice things. Wendell's all the time bringing her expensive stuff to make her happy."

"Well, Miss High-and-Mighty will be havin' Uncle Sam payin' for all her nice things now, I suppose."

Both women laughed.

"An' poor Wendell, maybe he'll realize once and for all that she's nothin' more than a murderin' whore. Maybe he'll be back to the nice, sweet Wendell he used to be."

"So you can have another crack at him. Ain't that right, Ty?"

"I told you before, LaVonne—that's all over with."

The women worked for a few minutes. It sounded to Claire as though one was scrubbing the floor while the other filled the paper-towel holders and soap dispensers.

"Have you talked to the police yet, Ty?"

"Not yet. How about you?"

"No. Maybe tomorrow."

"Maybe so. You just about finished with that?"

Claire didn't know why, but she held her breath. Obviously, the women hadn't noticed her way back in the end stall. But before she had a chance to decide what to do, the room was filled with voices. She could tell they were mystery fans. Then that bucket screeched across the floor again—she really hated that sound!—and LaVonne and Ty were gone.

The restaurant was crowded. The coffee shop was crowded. Even the snack bar near the pool was crowded. Claire stood near the shallow end, trying to decide what to do as she watched a father splash with his little boy. Should she wait in line at the coffee shop? Or should she try to find Gil and tell him about the conversation she had just overheard? Would the police be interested in what she'd found out, or did they already know? And if they knew, would they think she was interfering? Was she really hungry? While she stood there, she noticed a candy machine over by a Ping-Pong table.

It was a tough choice, but she went with the Mounds bar. Grabbing a Coke from the soda machine, she promised herself she'd eat a nutritious salad for dinner to make up for the vending-machine snack. Then she hurried back to the dealers' room.

CHAPTER 30

"WELL, WHAT YOU THINK?" Donovan asked Gil.

The detective had just finished questioning two mystery writers, the one who'd had ten novels published, and one who was famous for writing historical mysteries. Gil had watched and listened, never saying one word during either interview.

"Isn't it more important what you think?" Gil asked.

"I need your input here, Gil. I'm on the outside looking in."

"Okay. But tell me why you chose these two particular writers to question this morning?"

"Well . . . I asked around about who was competitive with this Westerly guy, and these two were the names I got."

"From whom?"

Donovan pursed his lips for a moment, then said, "I don't think I want to say."

"Okay, fine, protect your source," Gil said. "How come you've been using me right out in the open like this?"

"Why? Do you have anything to hide?"

"Of course not."

"Well, maybe my source does."

"And maybe your source is just using you. Maybe he has his own agenda," Gil said.

"What do you mean?"

"These two men you just interrogated, they hardly knew Robin Westerly. Why would they've had any kind of motive to kill him?"

"They were competitors, weren't they?" the detective asked.

"Detective," Gil explained, "these are midlist writers. This is not a dog-eat-dog business we're involved with here. Nobody'd move up a notch by killing Robin Westerly."

"I still don't understand," Donovan said. "Explain midlist."

"It's what we call mystery writers who are not enjoying the success of a Walter Mosley or Michael Connelly. They don't get large advances, and they don't get the push from their publishers the way the big boys do. Believe me, whoever killed Westerly had more of a motive than competition."

"Like what?"

"I don't know," Gil said. "You're the professional. Could it have been an accident?"

"Maybe."

"You know, I don't think I asked you this before," Gil said suddenly. "Why didn't anyone report hearing a shot?"

"With a single shot, people aren't always sure what they heard," Donovan said. "The gun that was used was a twenty-five; it's a small handgun, one that doesn't make much noise. And we're not certain that no one heard the shot. Maybe the maid did. That's one of the questions we're going to ask her when my men bring her in."

"I see."

Donovan checked his notepad, regarding it for a moment.

"Is that your list of suspects?" Gil asked.

"Some of them."

"Can I have a look?"

Donovan hesitated.

"You said you want my input, right?"

Donovan shrugged. "Right," he said, and handed it over.

For such a big man, Donovan had a small, childish scrawl. The only reason Gil was able to make out the names was that he was familiar with them.

"You've got two more writers on here like those you just spoke to. Interrogating them will be a waste of time."

"I think I should be the judge of that," Donovan said. "Don't you agree?"

"Hey," Gil said, "I'm just giving you my input. I could go back to my table in the dealers' room and be making some money right now."

"Okay, okay," Donovan said, "take it easy. So if I'll be wasting my time with those two, what about the names that are left?"

"It's logical to question them."

"Why's that?"

"Because one is Westerly's agent, and the other's his editor," Gil explained. "They know each other; they're more than just acquaintances who see each other at a convention once a year."

"Okay, that makes sense," Donovan said, reclaiming his notebook. "Now tell me which one this would be."

Gil looked at the doorway and saw Nicholas Ablow standing there. "That's Ablow. He is—or was—Westerly's agent."

"Mr. Ablow!" Donovan called, waving his arm. "Right here, please."

CHAPTER 31

NICHOLAS ABLOW WALKED to the table tentatively, taking oddly small steps for such a tall, gangly man. Donovan stood up as the man reached them.

"I'm Detective Donovan," he said, extending his hand, "I assume you know Gil Hunt?"

"Yes," Ablow said, slowly drawing his hand back from Donovan's vigorous shake. "May I ask what he's doing here?"

"Mr. Hunt is assisting me with my inquiries," Donovan said. "He's sort of my . . . guide through the mystery world. Have a seat, please."

Ablow didn't look happy about having Gil there, but he sat down. Because of his height and extreme slenderness, it seemed as if he folded himself into the chair.

"I have some questions about your client," Donovan said.

"Such a terrible tragedy, but I don't see what I can do to help."

"Well, you knew Mr. Westerly better than most people, didn't you?"

Warily, Ablow said, "Perhaps."

"Why don't I just ask the questions," Donovan suggested, "and you answer them to the best of your ability. How would that be?"

To Gil, it sounded as if the detective were talking to a reticent child. He knew Ablow to be a somewhat fussy but fairly sophisticated man. Why he wasn't balking at Donovan's tone surprised Gil.

"Very well," Ablow said. He crossed his legs and rested his hands in his lap, sitting away from the table. It appeared as if the man didn't want to bother having to push his chair away from the table when the time came to leave.

"What was Mr. Westerly's relationship with his wife like?"

"I'm sure I don't know," Ablow said. "You should ask his wife that."

"I did." Donovan didn't elaborate. "I want the opinion of an outsider."

Ablow hesitated, picked a piece of nonexistent lint from his trousers, and said, "They seemed . . . content."

"Content, or contentious?" Donovan asked.

"I don't know what you mean."

"Other people I've talked to said the two argued fairly often, and in public."

"I hadn't noticed."

Donovan stared at Ablow long enough for the agent to begin fidgeting.

"I don't think you're being very honest with me, sir," the detective said finally. "If other people had witnessed the couple fighting, surely you, who knew them on a more personal level, had seen it, as well."

"Oh, all right," Ablow said then, "so they argued. A lot of married couples do."

"What did they argue about?"

"Several things," Ablow said. "Robin didn't like the way Gloria tried to . . . direct his career. She was also not happy with the way her own writing was going."

"Are you representing her, as well?"

"I represented her on one matter as a favor to Robin."

"But you wouldn't say she was your client?"

"No, I wouldn't say that."

"All right," Donovan said, "let's move on. Who do you think might have held a grudge against Mr. Westerly?"

"A grudge? I think it more likely we're talking about jealousy here, Detective, not a grudge."

"Really? Enlighten me."

Gil thought Donovan's choice of words and phrases in talking with Ablow were meant to provoke the man, perhaps make the usually guarded agent drop his defenses. He'd watched Donovan interrogate three men so far, and he thought the detective was very good at his job—or at least this portion of it. On the whole, the persona Donovan seemed bent on displaying struck Gil as being a bit Columboesque.

"Robin is—was—an award-winning author. He was on the verge of great things."

"Such as?"

"I believe he would have cracked the bestseller lists with his next book . . . or possibly the one after that."

Gil knew Ablow was exaggerating. Robin Westerly's books were nowhere near making the bestseller lists and, as a bookseller, Gil had never seen greatness in the man's future. The author had gotten excellent reviews, but they had not often translated into sales. He had a core readership, but it didn't go much beyond that.

"So you think this caused some others to become jealous?"

"Of course."

"Jealous enough to kill him?"

"I'm sure I don't know," Ablow said. "I am simply trying to answer your questions to the best of my ability."

Gil hid a smile. It was obvious the agent was now attempting to handle the detective. He suspected Ablow was a shrewd negotiator. Watching them was much more interesting than watching Donovan question the previous two men had been.

"And I appreciate that, sir."

Donovan questioned Ablow for ten minutes more, but Gil couldn't see that the detective had learned anything important from the man.

"All right, Mr. Ablow," Donovan said finally, "I think that's all for now. I appreciate your coming by and talking to me."

Ablow stood up, taking a moment to adjust the drape of his suit jacket. "I assume you have a few suspects?"

"On the contrary, Mr. Ablow, I have an entire hotelful."

Gil had the feeling the agent wanted to ask if that included him, but in the end the man simply nodded at both of them, turned, and used a long, purposeful stride to take his leave.

"What did you learn from that?" Gil asked.

"That Mr. Ablow is probably a good agent," Donovan said. "What did you learn?"

"That he has an exaggerated opinion of the importance of his client."

"And, by extension, of himself, probably."

"That's a given."

"Where is he from?" Donovan asked. "It sounded like he was trying to hide an accent."

"Australia, I think. I not sure, though."

Donovan thought a moment, then said, "You're probably right. I can see that."

"Who's next?" Gil asked.

"Well, according to you, I'd be wasting my time talking to the other writers, but I think I'll do it anyway. And, of course, the editor. Is that the same as the publisher?"

"Generally speaking," Gil said, "when people talk about a publisher, they mean the company, and the editor works for the company."

"I see," Donovan said. "You're really being very helpful, Gil. I don't know about you, but I could use a break. Why don't we meet back here in ten minutes?"

"Fine." Gil hadn't noticed it before, but now that he had watched Donovan talk with Ablow, he had the feeling the detective used much the same tone with him.

Suddenly, he felt like a suspect himself.

CHAPTER 32

DURING THE BREAK, Gil felt he should go to the dealers' room and tell Claire what was going on. He didn't want her to think he'd just abandoned her. He took the elevator down to the lobby, but when the doors opened, he was intercepted by Lowell Fleming before he could walk ten feet.

Fleming was Dave Spenser's co-organizer for the convention. While Spense was from Seattle, Fleming was local, an Omaha book dealer with a Book Den franchise. It wasn't a mystery bookstore, but Fleming did have a huge mystery section, which he kept well stocked. Gil had only met Fleming at a convention the year before. Spense and Fleming were there plugging this Omaha event.

"Gil Hunt!" Fleming said, stopping short as he was crossing the lobby. "Just the man I was looking for."

"Hi, Lowell. Why were you looking for me?"

"I need your help."

Gil couldn't believe how in demand he was. Since meeting Claire Duncan, all he'd wanted to do was spend time with her, get to know her, but apparently that wasn't meant to be.

"Lowell, I really have to be—"

"Look, Gil, I know Spense is your friend." His tone was amazingly accusatory.

"What are you talking about?"

"I think he's gone off the deep end, what with this murder and all. He's never around when I need him."

"I thought you guys were co-organizers? You don't need him to make decisions, do you?"

"He's the one with the contacts," Fleming said. "He's the one who knows all the writers personally. And he's the one who planned most of the events. I did a lot of the scut work here in town—you know, dealing with the hotel, getting book bags and giveaways."

"So what's the problem?"

"I need him to pull his end here. That's the problem," Fleming said. "He's the one with the checkbook—I got people screaming to be paid, things I have to go out and buy. Do you have any idea where he is right now?"

"Uh, no, I don't, but—"

"Well, neither do I." The man looked ready to tear his hair out, and with the receding hairline he was sporting, that would not have been a good thing.

"Look, Lowell, if I see Spense, I'll tell him you're looking for him." Gil started to walk away, but Fleming grabbed his arm.

"I'm sorry," Fleming said when he realized what he had done. He released Gil's arm immediately. "If you see him, could you talk to him? Calm him down? I mean, I know the murder was a terrible thing, but it hasn't increased our attendance as much as Spense said it would, and frankly, I'm the one who's about to lose it here, Gil."

"Spense said the murder would increase attendance?" Gil asked. "When was this?"

"Right after it happened. I guess he was looking for a silver lining, you know? But there isn't one."

"Attendance is that bad?"

"Apparently, Westerly was not a very good choice for guest of honor," Fleming said. "He just didn't pack them in the way we thought he would. Frankly, I didn't think asking him was a good idea. I mean, my customers really don't like those historicals he writes, but Spense was insistent."

No wonder Spense has been going crazy, Gil thought. He pushes for Westerly to be guest of honor and the man doesn't draw—dead or alive.

"Okay," Gil said, "I'm sorry, Lowell. I'll find Spense and talk to him."

"Thanks. I've got a couple of authors who aren't on panels and I don't know where to put them."

Gil wanted to get to the dealers' room, but Fleming's dilemma really seemed to have the man frustrated.

"Do you have a schedule with you?"

"Uh, yeah, sure . . ." Fleming pulled one from his pocket.

"Who are the authors? Maybe I can help."

As luck would have it, Gil knew the authors' work and, although he didn't know them personally, was able to suggest to Fleming a couple of panels where he could add the writers.

"Wow," Fleming said, "thanks a lot. You saved my life. I'll find these guys and tell them what's going on."

"Glad to help—and when I see Spense, I'll have a talk with him."

"That would be great." He smiled weakly. "Maybe I'll make it through this whole thing in one piece after all."

"I'm sure you will."

Fleming went one way, and as Gil prepared to head for

the dealers' room, the elevator doors opened and Detective Donovan stepped out.

"Hey, Gil," he called. "Break time's over."

Gil looked at his watch. It was more than three hours since he'd left Claire in the dealers' room. He only hoped she wouldn't get angry and leave.

CHAPTER 33

GIL SAT through the interrogation of two more writers, but he could tell that Donovan had taken his advice. The detective's heart just wasn't in it, and he held each of the men for only a few minutes.

But that wasn't the case with Westerly's editor.

Barry Newcomb was a senior editor at Oak Mill Press, but there were many senior editors in the business. In truth, the man had very little in the way of pull. Newcomb was thirty-five, and he had been a regular at these conventions for about seven years. Gil knew a few of Newcomb's other authors, and none of them was very impressed with his editorial abilities.

"Thanks for coming, Mr. Newcomb," Donovan said. "I'm sure you know Mr. Hunt."

"Yes, hello, Gil."

"Barry."

Gil had been on a panel with Newcomb a couple of years before when someone had wanted to put together a book dealer, an editor, a critic, and two writers to discuss serial-killer books. Gil found that

Newcomb's knowledge of the subgenre was severely lacking.

"I assume you're pretty upset about Mr. Westerly's murder?"

"*Upset?*" Newcomb asked. "Shocked is more like it. And when I called my boss in New York, he was appalled."

"Why?" Donovan asked. "I mean, wouldn't his books sell better now that he's dead? You could republish them all and make more money."

"First of all," Newcomb said, "it doesn't work that way. These are books, not priceless works of art. Second, we don't own his complete backlist."

Donovan looked at Gil.

"Backlist just means all his previously published books."

"I see," Donovan said.

"We were in the process of negotiating for them, almost had them, too."

"What happened? His agent queer the deal?"

"His agent?" Newcomb asked. "The man who would be Dominick Abel?"

Again, Donovan looked at Gil for an explanation.

"Mr. Abel is considered the agent to the stars in the mystery field," Gil said.

"And Ablow is not Abel." Newcomb said. "It's kind of a joke in the industry. Anyway, no, it wasn't his agent who tossed a monkey wrench into the works. It was his wife. So we were still in negotiation, and now this."

"What about his new book?"

"He was still working on it," Newcomb said. "It's months late. Now we'll probably never get it."

"So, with him dead, your company is screwed."

"Definitely."

"And on a personal level? You've lost a friend?"

"Hardly," the editor said. "He was hell to work with, and his wife was worse."

"You publish her, as well?"

"No, but she literally runs—or ran—his career."

"I thought that was his agent's job."

"So did his agent," Newcomb said. "The two of them never really got along. In fact, I wouldn't have been surprised if at some point he'd fired his agent and allowed his wife to represent him."

"Was there a danger of that?"

"A distinct possibility, if I'm any judge."

"And you two weren't friends?"

"No," Newcomb said. "I don't find it wise to become friendly with my authors."

"Well, would you have any idea who would want to kill him?"

"No," Newcomb said, "I really didn't know him that well."

"But . . . you worked with him?"

"I got his manuscripts, edited them, sent them back in the mail for changes—not that he'd make them willingly."

"What about negotiations?"

"That would go on between me and the agent," Newcomb said. "So you see, I can't help you with any personal information."

Gil had been watching Newcomb closely the whole time he was talking. The man seemed nervous, while, as Gil recalled, in the past he had always projected an air of calm, and an arrogance born of ignorance. He was the kind of man who thought he was cool but didn't have a clue what it actually took to be cool. In Gil's neighborhood in New York, they would have said a guy like Newcomb "thinks who he is." And he usually put on a good show—but not today.

"I don't think Mr. Newcomb can help you further, Detective Donovan."

Donovan looked at Gil, who had kept silent through most of the meetings that morning, and frowned.

Gil shrugged. "Hey, that's my input."

Donovan hesitated, then said, "All right." He looked at the editor. "Thank you for your time, Mr. Newcomb."

Newcomb stood up. "I hope you catch the bastard who did it. He's costing me no end of trouble, not to mention money."

Donovan waited until Newcomb had left the room, then turned to Gil. "What was that all about?"

"Something wasn't right about him. He seemed too nervous."

"Do you think talking to a police detective might have had something to do with that?"

Briefly, Gil explained what he knew about Newcomb's personality.

"I know people like that," Donovan said. "I guess I'll have to find out what made Mr. Newcomb so nervous."

"Are we done here?" Gil asked.

"Yep." Donovan pushed his chair away from the table. "Thanks for your help, Gil. I may be calling on you again."

"I hope not."

"Why?"

Gil stood up. "I don't like being used."

"What makes you think I'm using you?"

"I've watched you talk to all these people this morning."

The detective cocked his head to the side. "And?"

"And you were handling them."

"What's your point?"

"You've been talking to me the same way," Gil said. "You've been handling me, haven't you?"

The two men regarded each other for a few moments, and then Donovan said, "I've been doing my job, Mr. Hunt."

"Mr. Hunt? Not on a first-name basis anymore. Should my feelings be hurt?"

Donovan smiled. "Thanks again."

Gil stood there as Donovan left the room, marveling at how he'd stood up to the detective. After all, he wasn't a private eye; he was just a bookstore owner.

CHAPTER 34

THIS TIME, Gil made it across the lobby of the hotel before he was stopped.

"Hey, dude," mystery writer Percy Parker called out. "Not used to seein' you out of the dealers' room."

Parker was a transplanted Chicagoan, now living in Las Vegas. Gil had met him at a convention in Chicago almost twenty-five years ago. After all those years, the man's ebony skin was still smooth and unblemished, but his hair was now streaked with gray.

"Hey, Percy, it's good to see you." The two men shared a warm handshake.

"I went by your table, but you weren't there," Percy said. "Saw a pretty lady, though. Friend of yours?"

"A new friend," Gil said, then added, "At least I hope she's still feeling friendly toward me. I've left her sitting there all day."

"What's this I hear about you bein' involved in that Westerly murder? Man, imagine that, murder at a mystery convention."

"I found the body; that's all."

"Folks are sayin' you're workin' on the case. When did you become a detective?"

"It's a long story, Percy, and I've got to get back. I'll tell you about it some other time, okay?"

"Sure, but I'm only lettin' you go because I saw that lady you're rushin' off to see. We'll catch up later."

"Thanks," Gil said. He slapped his friend on the back and rushed off toward the dealers' room.

Wendell Payne knew Gil Hunt's business was selling books, so he decided to wait for him in the hall by the door to the dealers' room. He'd finally talked Graciella into trusting somebody other than him with her story. Now all he had to do was talk Gil into being that somebody.

"Hey, Wendell."

The big black man turned to see a bellman bearing down on him.

"What's up, Hank?" he asked the man.

"Bell captain's been lookin' for you," Hank said.

"Damn! I got somethin' important on, Hank. Can you cover for me?

"I guess so, but where do I tell him you are?"

"Tell him you didn't see me. I'll explain it all later."

"Okay," Hank said, "it's your ass on the line, not mine."

Wendell turned back toward the dealers' room just in time to spot Gil walking in. Thankfully, the distraction hadn't caused him to miss the man.

"Mr. Hunt!" he called, rushing forward.

Gil heard his name and closed his eyes. He'd almost made it! He considered not stopping, but when he turned, he saw Wendell Payne and was glad for the chance to speak to him.

"Wendell," he said. "I've been looking for you."

"And I've been looking for you, sir. Have you got a few minutes? I need to take you someplace so we can talk."

"What's wrong with right here?"

Wendell looked around. "Too many people," he said. "And I especially don't want that detective cornin' by."

"You don't want to run into Detective Donovan?"

"No, sir, I don't!"

"Why?"

"I'll tell you that outside. Please, Mr. Hunt, it's very important."

"Wendell, I really should get back to my table," Gil said, pointing in Claire's direction.

But the man was insistent. "Please, sir, it's a matter of life and death."

Gil didn't know if Wendell was just being melodramatic.

He looked across the room and could see Claire talking to a customer. So close, he thought. He waited a second, hoping she'd glance his way so he could at least wave. But she didn't.

When he looked back at Wendell, it was the fearful expression on his face that made Gil finally give in.

"Okay, but we'll have to make it quick."

"I can't tell you how much I appreciate this. Thank you, sir," Wendell said, leading the way down the hall.

CHAPTER 35

CLAIRE HAD HAD a difficult time maneuvering through the groups of enthusiastic conventiongoers. By the time she had reached Gil's table, she'd convinced herself that he would be sitting there, patiently waiting for her. But when she'd arrived, everything was as she had left it.

"Can you cover for me now?" the dealer at the next table asked. "If I don't have a cigarette, I'll scream."

"Sure," Claire said, taking a bite out of her candy bar.

"Gil's sure lucky to have you. And happier than I've ever seen him."

"Really?"

"You two are good together."

Claire smiled to herself as the woman walked away, buttoning her cardigan.

When she finished the last of her soda, Claire checked her watch. Gil had been gone three hours. Life with him—so far—had certainly not been dull.

An elderly man approached her. "Do you have any Robin Westerly books?" he asked. "And if they're signed, even better."

Claire was unfamiliar with Gil's inventory and surprised it was the first time all day someone had asked for one of Westerly's books.

"If we do, they'd be in that section." She pointed, remembering Gil had told a customer yesterday where the new releases were.

"Can't see it," the man said, putting on his glasses. "Nope, I don't see one."

She stood up to go around the table and look for herself, when she spotted Gil across the room. He was talking to someone and didn't appear to be very happy with the conversation.

"Maybe you have one behind the table?" the man asked.

"No." Her attention momentarily snapped back to the customer. "We don't keep any stock back there."

When she looked toward Gil again, she saw the person he was talking to was Wendell Payne.

Her body started to move forward without any help from her brain. And she was around the table before she realized she couldn't leave Gil's stock unattended, not to mention the items at the adjoining table.

"Guess I'll keep looking," the man said when he realized Claire wasn't paying any attention to him.

"Guess so. Sorry."

Claire waved in Gil's direction, hoping to catch his eye, but he was standing at such an angle that he couldn't see her.

Wendell looked frightened. To see the large man that way made her feel sad for him, even from that distance, despite the fact she didn't know him. The more they talked, the more animated Gil became. After a few moments, he pointed in her direction, shaking his head the whole time. His whole demeanor gave her the impression that he was talking about his table, the convention, that nothing they were saying involved her.

And then abruptly, the two men walked out of the room.

Claire went after them. Before she could give herself more reasons to stay, she ran.

They were walking at a clipped pace. It didn't seem that Gil had been coerced into going with Wendell. Their voices were low and the distance she was from them kept her from hearing a single word.

They were headed for the lobby. She stayed behind, waiting for a sign—something, anything, that would cue her to run to help Gil.

When they walked out the front entrance and into the brilliant sunlight, she stayed with them. Wendell unlocked the passenger side of a van and Gil got in willingly. Wendell walked around to the driver's side and Claire waited for them to drive away, trying all the while to figure out if she was angry for being left out or just angry with herself for standing there in the parking lot like a fool.

"So, Wendell, why here? What's so important that you had to drag me outside?"

Wendell Payne ran his large hand over the top of his bald head. Perspiration glistened on his brow. "Sorry, Mr. Hunt. . . ."

"Relax. Call me Gil."

"Thank you, sir, but no. I need advice right now—not a friend. I need to feel we're doing official, uh, police business here. . . ."

"But Wendell, I'm not with the police."

"As close as you can get without being one of them, I suppose."

Gil was surprised to realize Wendell thought of him that way. "I just happened to be the guy who found a dead body. The first person—"

"I know Detective Donovan told you I live with Graciella Sanchez. And I also know he told you that she was the maid in the room with Mr. Westerly. It was Graciella you saw there that night."

Gil held up his hand. "Hold on. Donovan told me his men were going to your place to question Graciella today. By now, they've probably left, and when you get home, she'll fill you in. So there's really no reason for us—"

"The police aren't going to find Gracie there when they come round. She left."

"Left you? Or the city?" Gil asked.

"Neither."

"I don't get it. Where is she, then?"

"Oh, she wanted to take off, leave the country all together. But I stopped her. I told her it would look bad. And Mr. Hunt," Wendell said in his sincerest voice, "that girl just happened to be in the wrong place at the wrongest time. She didn't do nuthin', Mr. Hunt. She's a decent girl."

"So she'll tell the police her story, they'll take her statement, and she'll have nothing to worry about."

Wendell held back a laugh. "If you think that's the way it works, you have a hell of a lot to learn. People like us, especially like Gracie, someone from another country all together, don't get treated the same way as people like you. No disrespect intended, Mr. Hunt."

"Wendell, just because I've never been arrested doesn't mean I don't know there are problems with the legal system, but—"

"We can talk about problems another time, sir. Right now, I need for you to come with me and talk to Gracie."

Gil sat there stunned. "Why would you want me to do that?"

"Because you're a decent man. You'll listen to Gracie and go to the police on her behalf. And mostly because you saw her. She didn't have no blood on her, did she?"

"No."

"And killin' someone is messy business. Am I right?"

"Yes. From everything I know about forensics, there would have to be some trace of blood on her." But, Gil thought, it could be microscopic.

"She stood there in her white uniform. She didn't touch nuthin'. Not the gun, not the body. The cops will see that her fingerprints ain't on nuthin' when they do all their tests."

"They don't have the murder weapon, Wendell." As soon as Gil mentioned that detail, he regretted it. Donovan hadn't sworn him to secrecy, but he assumed it was a fact the detective didn't want leaked.

"How far away from here is she?" Gil asked.

"'Bout ten minutes. Not far. I'll have you back in an hour, tops."

"Look, Wendell, let me call Detective Donovan. He seems like a fair, honest man."

"No, Mr. Hunt. Please. First you talk to Gracie. She's real scared. I figured that maybe if you just listen to what she has to say—let her get everything off her chest—she'll feel better and we can convince her to talk to the police."

Gil looked through the side window, scanning the area while trying to figure out what he should do. Maybe he was being stupid, but he trusted Wendell and believed every word he had said. But if he went with the man, he should tell someone, just to be safe. Taking a business card out of his pocket, he jotted down a message for Claire. "Give me a minute," he told Wendell. "I'll be right back."

"I'll be here waitin'. And Mr. Hunt? Thanks."

Gil got out of the van and ran inside to leave the card at the front desk. "Could you please page Claire Duncan and give her this message?" he asked.

CHAPTER 36

GRACIELLA PACED. This was a bad idea. She should have never let Wendell talk her into staying. The loading dock was so quiet on the weekend. She walked to a pallet piled with soft bundles of clean towels wrapped in brown paper and sat down. The Sparkling Clean Laundry serviced all major hotels in the area. While she had spent almost a year putting their clean sheets on hundreds of beds and folding and unfolding the towels they recycled, she had never been to this part of their operation before. At least the place smelled clean, not like some of the warehouses she'd worked in.

When the van pulled up, she was trying to decide how much more of her day to waste. She watched through dirty windows as Wendell parked between two delivery trucks. When he got out, her first impulse was to run into his arms. She always felt safe there. But then she saw the other man and stayed where she was.

She watched as they walked into the side door leading to the office, then sat very quietly while Wendell called her name. There's still time to run, she told herself. Just hide until they're gone.

"Graciella! Come on, baby, I know you're here!"

But where would she go?

"Are you out there?" Wendell yelled, and then spotted her. She nodded.

The other man walked behind Wendell. When they were in front of her, she couldn't meet their eyes with hers.

"Hi, Graciella, I'm Gil Hunt."

"I know who you are."

"Don't be like that, Gracie. Mr. Hunt's come out here to help us."

"You mean *me*, don't you? The way I see it, you're fine."

Wendell looked at Gil, embarrassed.

Gil looked at his watch.

The tension finally broke her and she stood up, glaring at Wendell, then glancing over shyly at Gil.

Being so close to her brought back that night, and he instantly recognized her as the woman at the murder scene.

Wendell put his arms around her. "Come on, we can use the office. Jimmy said it would be okay."

"And Jimmy is?" Gil asked.

"Jimmy Lewison, my cousin's best friend. I've known him since high school. He's cool with us usin' his place."

Claire read Gil's note, turned the card over, then back again, rereading the words. "This is it?" she asked the man at the front desk.

"Yes, ma'am."

"Mr. Hunt gave this to you himself?"

"Yes, ma'am."

"Was there anyone with him?"

"No."

"And when was that?"

"All I know is, he walked in here about fifteen minutes ago, handed me the card, and asked that I page you and give it to you."

"I'm sorry but it's just . . ." The man rolled his eyes when he thought she wasn't looking at him. She wanted to scream her frustration in his direction, but instead she just put the card in her pocket and said, "Thank you."

Claire mumbled to herself, a habit she hated, as she walked back once again to the dealers' room. The day was turning out to be such a strange one. But then, what had she expected? Someone had been murdered in the hotel and that horrible crime had set the tone for the convention.

"Everything okay?" the dealer next to her asked.

"Fine."

Claire passed the time reading a magazine in between sales. Her stomach grumbled, but she was too upset to eat.

"Mrs. Duncan?" Claire looked up and saw Detective Donovan standing in front of her.

"Hi, Detective."

"You're helping out Mr. Hunt, then?"

"That's right, and it seems to be turning into an all-day job," she said.

"Where is he?" Donovan asked, looking down the aisle.

"I don't know, and to tell you the truth, I'm worried about him."

"We finished our interviews a little while ago. He's probably on his way down right now."

She debated with herself how much to tell him, then decided that of all the people she should be honest with, it should be a police detective.

"Well, I saw him a few minutes ago, standing across the room there. I thought he was coming back here, but he stopped to talk to a man."

"What man?"

"His name is Wendell," she replied. "He works here in the hotel."

"Wendell Payne," Donovan said, cutting her off. "I know who he is."

"I was worried for a while that he was stalking Gil, and now they've gone off together—left the hotel."

"Left? I think you'd better tell me everything, Mrs. Duncan."

"Well," she said, "they went down the hall and I followed . . ."

"And he got into the van willingly?" Donovan asked when she was finished.

"That's the way it looked to me."

"The other man didn't push him, force him in any way? Did it seem as if Gil might have had a gun held on him?"

"No," Claire said. "He got into the van on his own."

Donovan looked down at the card in his hand and read the message aloud. "'Back soon. Don't be mad. Now I owe you much more chocolate and junk jewelry.'" It was signed "Gil." "Doesn't sound like a very big spender to me," Donovan said.

"Oh, that's just a private joke," she said, rushing to Gil's defense, and then suddenly she felt her cheeks burning. "Could he be in danger?" she asked.

"He might be. This Wendell lives with the maid you and Gil found with Westerly's body; I sent some men to her place to question her, but she's gone missing."

"And now Wendell has Gil? I don't understand."

"Neither do I," he said, "but I intend to."

He stood there, seemingly lost in thought for a moment, tapping the card against a fingernail. Oddly, it very quickly became unbearable to Claire, sounding like an anvil being hammered in her head. "Can I have that back before you spring into action?" she asked.

"Huh? Oh, of course." He returned the card to her. "Don't worry, Mrs. Hunt, I'll find him."

As Donovan strode away, she realized that he'd accidentally called her Mrs. Hunt, and her cheeks burned again.

CHAPTER 37

THE MOMENT WAS AN AWKWARD ONE. Both Gil and Graciella looked at Wendell, waiting for him to take the lead. After all, it was because of him the three now found themselves at the warehouse.

"Look, Mr. Hunt, Gracie didn't kill that writer back at the hotel."

"Then why doesn't she go and tell the police that?"

"The police?" she said with contempt. "The police don't care who killed Mr. Westerly. I'm just an easy mark for them to arrest, because you saw me there."

"Gracie—"

"Yeah, yeah, I know," she said, waving a hand at the big man. "It ain't his fault; it ain't my fault. It's nobody's fault."

Obviously, the woman was bitter about something. But it seemed to Gil her bitterness predated the murder.

"Grace—can I call you Gracie?"

"Whatever."

"Why don't you calmly tell me what happened, in your own words"—he gave a cautionary look toward Wendell —"and I'll pass it on to the police."

"Mr. Hunt, I don't see what you can—"

"Gracie, honey," Wendell pleaded. "Please, just talk to the man." She turned her head for a moment, seemed to be staring at the nudie calendar on the wall, although Gil doubted she was even seeing it.

Wendell had invited Gil to seat himself behind Jimmy's desk and had then directed Gracie to sit across from him. He remained standing. Wendell was so big, he made the small room seem even smaller.

"Grace?"

She jerked her head back and her long dark hair fell away from her eyes. "All right! I heard a sound," she said. "I was cleaning the room next door, and I heard a . . . commotion."

"What kind of commotion?" Gil asked.

"At first it sounded like an argument," she said. "You know, two people yelling at each other."

"Could you make out what they were saying?"

"No," she said, "I just knew there were voices."

"Okay, did you hear, two men? A man and a woman?"

She thought a moment, then said, "Two men. I'm sure they were both men's voices."

"And then what?"

"I heard a sound. Like a shot."

"Have you ever heard a gunshot before?" Gil asked.

She gave him a look and said, "Mister, you have got to be kidding. Where I come from, lots of people been shot at —including me. Yeah, I know the kinda sound a gun makes. All right?"

Gil, who had never been shot at in his life, bowed to her superior knowledge. "Go on."

"After that, I didn't hear nuthin', so I decided to go next door and have a look."

"That was brave of you."

"Curious, not brave. Stupid, not brave. And dumb, 'cause I still had to clean that damn room."

"You clean in the evening?" Gil asked. "I thought all that was done by late afternoon."

"The heavy stuff. But at that time, we're turning down beds, making sure there's enough towels, cleaning up accidents. You know."

Gil nodded. "So then you went next door and you let yourself in?"

"I didn't have to," she said. "It was open—but not all the way."

"Ajar?"

"Yeah, ajar." She shook her head, agitated at Gil's preciseness. "So . . . I knocked, and when there was no answer, I went in."

"Did you pull the door closed behind you?"

"You don't have to," she said. "Those doors slam shut all by themselves."

"She's right about that, Mr. Hunt," Wendell said.

"Okay, so what did you do next?" Gil asked.

"Well . . . he was there on the floor," she said, waving and looking down at the floor of the office, as if the dead man were sprawled out there at that very moment.

"Dead?"

"I . . . didn't know. I never saw so much blood before. I didn't touch him . . . I couldn't. And then you came in with the lady . . . and the others behind you."

"Then you ran when I asked you what had happened."

She took her eyes from the floor and looked at him. "I panicked," she said. "I didn't even know I was running until I was halfway down the hall." A tear fell from one eye and she brushed it away harshly with her palm.

"Had you cleaned that room before?"

"Of course. That's my section of the floor. I clean that room all the time."

"No, I meant after Mr. and Mrs. Westerly checked in."

"Oh, well, yes, once. In fact, I knocked on the door the morning before, and the woman yelled at me."

"Yelled?"

"She shouted through the door for me to go away."

"Did you hear any other yelling from inside?"

Gracie hesitated. Gil looked at Wendell, who shrugged his big round shoulders.

"Gracie," Gil said, "I don't care if you listened at the door. You're not going to get in trouble for that."

"Yeah," she said reluctantly, "I guess bein' suspected of murder is worse than losin' my job."

"Grace—" Wendell began.

"I'm talkin' to him, Wendell, ain't I?" she snapped.

The big man got a hurt look on his face and fell silent. It occurred to Gil that Wendell was completely under the woman's thumb. She was pretty, sexy even, with her dark hair and eyes, something he certainly had not noticed the only other time he'd seen her. It was surprising to him then that Wendell had even been able to convince her to do anything—let alone talk to him.

"Gracie?" he prompted, and waited for her reply.

CHAPTER 38

"OKAY," she said to Gil, "so I listened at the door. They weren't shoutin', but they were definitely arguin'."

"And did you go back later to clean the room?"

"Yeah, after they left."

"Did you run into either of them after that? Around the hotel somewhere?"

"The next day—the morning of the murder. I came to the room again, at my usual time. You know, if you folks don't want me knocking on your door, then put out the DO NOT DISTURB sign. That's what it's there for. It's not as if—"

Gil interrupted her tirade. "So you knocked again?"

"Yes. This time, the man opened the door and told me real snotty like to come back later. Actually, his wife said it. She was standing behind him and said, 'Tell the bitch to come back later.'"

"What did he say?"

"He said, 'You heard my wife. Later!' and slammed the door right in my face."

Gil wondered what Donovan would have asked next.

"So that was it? You didn't see either of them again after that until you found Mr. Westerly dead?"

"That's right."

"Did you see anything strange in the room when you found him?" he asked. "Something that might help the police?"

She hesitated and something shifted in her eyes, something that made him feel she was lying when she answered. "No. I didn't have time to notice nuthin'. That's when you came in."

Gil looked at Wendell and received the same shrug as before. "Gracie, do you want to tell this to the police?"

"Wendell thinks I should."

"What do you think?"

"I think they'll arrest me," she said.

"Why?"

"Because it'll be easy. I'm not from this country."

"That's not enough of a reason for them to arrest anyone."

"No?" Her eyes flashed. "Have you dealt with the police before?"

"Well," he admitted, "I haven't had much reason to—"

"Well, I have!" she said. "As a woman, especially as an immigrant, I have no reason to put much confidence in your police."

"Gracie, let me take you to Detective Donovan; he's the man in charge. He seems fair; I know he'll listen to you."

Grace hesitated, then said sullenly, "I don't know. I have to think about it."

"All right," Gil said, "I can understand that. But can you at least tell me where you're staying?"

"No. I don't trust you . . . not yet."

"Grace—" Wendell began, but this time it was Gil who quieted him by holding up his hand.

"That's all right. I understand." Gil wondered if Grace would have been more comfortable with another woman. "Can we meet here again tomorrow night? It'll give you time to think about things. You can decide if you're ready to talk to the police. Okay?"

Sunday was the last day of the convention—by Sunday night, most of the attendees would be gone. Gil thought about Donovan and what he would do concerning the people leaving before his case had been solved.

"Gracie, baby, he's only tryin' to help you," Wendell said.

Gil braced himself for another biting remark from the woman, but it didn't come.

"All right. Yes, I'll meet you here tomorrow."

"Good," Gil said.

It got awkward again as he waited for one of them to make a move.

"Good," Wendell said finally, clapping his hands together, "that's settled, then. Come on, Mr. Hunt, I'll drive you back to the hotel."

"I'll see you here at the same time, Gracie," Gil said. "I hope you'll decide to trust me and let me try to do more to help you."

When she didn't reply, Gil looked at Wendell, who led him out of the office.

When they reached the van, Wendell stopped before getting in.

"Thanks for cornin' to see her, Mr. Hunt."

Gil didn't point out that he hadn't really been given much choice.

"Do you think she'll agree to go to the police?" he asked.

"I sure hope so."

"Do you think she'll do anything foolish, Wendell, like running away?"

Wendell hesitated, then said, "I don't think so. See, we're together. I don't think she'd go anywhere without me."

"I hope you're right."

It was starting to get chilly, and as Gil zipped up his jacket, he said, "I was thinking she might respond better to another woman. She doesn't seem to have a very high opinion of men . . . or of the police, for that matter."

"That might work," Wendell said, unlocking the doors. "But who would you bring?"

Gil was thinking of Claire, but he didn't know if he'd dare ask her. By the time he got back to the hotel, she might not even be speaking to him anymore.

"I don't know," he said. "Why don't we get back to the hotel so I can work on it."

"Right."

They both got into the van, but before Wendell could start the engine, Gil asked, "Does Graciella have her own transportation?"

He nodded. "She has a car."

There were several cars in the lot, which Gil assumed belonged to the business, or the owner. "Do you know where she's staying?"

"Yes, sir, but I don't think it would be right for me to tell you."

"I understand," Gil said. "So I guess we're done here for today."

"Yes, sir," Wendell said, "I guess we are."

CHAPTER 39

GIL FOUND out later that after Donovan left the dealers' room, he went to the lobby to question the bell captain, Frank Winston, about Wendell. In Donovan's mind, Wendell had stepped up to become a major suspect, and if he had kidnapped Gil Hunt, there might be another murder in the offing.

"Wendell's real reliable," Frank said, "or at least he used to be."

"What happened?"

"Graciella happened," Frank said. "As soon as the hotel hired her, Wendell changed. He got one sniff of that Spanish snatch—pardon my French—and that was all she wrote. He started chasin' her right away."

"And did he catch her?"

"Sure did," the gray-haired older man said. "They're a couple, even got a place together."

"Did Wendell come to work today?"

"That guy never misses a day—which makes what he did this morning sorta strange."

"And what did he do?" Donovan asked.

"He disappeared on me." Frank was a black man with sad eyes, which were even sadder at the moment. "That boy was headed for my job. I'm due to retire shortly, and he was next in line. But after this—"

"What do you mean he disappeared?"

"Just what I said. One of the other boys, Hank, told Wendell I needed him, but Wendell said he had something important to do and asked Hank to cover for him. Fact is, I saw Wendell a few minutes after that, rushin' through the lobby with another fella, a white fella I think is a guest. I started to call him, but they run out the door too fast. I ain't seen him since."

"Okay," Donovan said, "thanks."

He moved away from the bell captain's station, took out his cell phone, and keyed in the number of his partner's phone.

"Jerry? Yeah. I got a situation, here. That maid we're looking for? Looks like her boyfriend may have grabbed Gil Hunt."

"Hunt?" Jerry Lyle asked. "That the book dealer you've been working with?"

"That's him. The guy we're looking for is Wendell Payne. Left here with Hunt less than an hour ago."

"Did Payne take him against his will?"

"Not sure. I got a witness who says no, but I don't know how reliable she is. Take some uniforms back out to that house. Turns out he and the maid are shacked up together. Have them canvass the area, see if anyone's spotted him."

"What are you gonna do?"

"I'll stay here. If he happens to come back here, I'm gonna collar Payne and have a little chat with him. Maybe being cuffed will persuade him to talk."

"May not be the first time for him, partner."

"I know," Donovan said, "but we'll see. Anyway, send me some backup. This dude's a big guy, and if he resists arrest, I'm gonna need help to take him down."

"You got it. Be careful."

"Aren't I always?"

Donovan killed the connection, turned around, and saw Claire Duncan coming across the lobby toward him. She did not look happy.

CHAPTER 40

IT TOOK ten minutes for Claire to mull over her conversation with Detective Donovan and get good and frustrated. The more she thought about it, the more it seemed Donovan hadn't reacted properly to the information she'd given him. Granted, she was not a cop, or even a mystery writer, but she was a very logical person. Her logic and good common sense had always gotten her through the rough spots. And now it seemed obvious to her that Wendell taking Gil away from the hotel the way he had should have set off some sort of cop alarm in Donovan's head. It was logical to her that if Wendell was involved with the maid and now she was missing, and then he had become involved with Gil, who was missing, too, that made Wendell Payne a very suspicious character—no matter how many nice things Gil had to say about him.

She waited as long as she could, but then her frustration started calling the shots. She had to find Donovan and make sure he understood what was happening and did something about it—now. And this thing that was going on between her and Gil Hunt, whether it was romantic or platonic, she certainly wanted to find out about it. And she couldn't do that if he was . . . dead.

She turned to the dealer nearest her and asked, "Could you please tell me what you have to do to close out a table?"

Claire saw Donovan in the lobby of the hotel; he was talking on his cell phone. She crossed the floor just as he was breaking the connection. When he saw her, he looked surprised.

"Mrs. Duncan—"

"What are you doing about finding Gil?" she demanded.

"Well, ma'am, I'm—"

"Don't 'ma'am' me, detective. And don't patronize me and tell me you'll handle everything. I gave you a critical piece of information. Gil has been taken away—maybe kidnapped—by someone who should be your number-one suspect, and you act as if all you can do is stand here and wait until he walks back through the front door . . . all by himself."

"Mrs.—"

"And just for the record, I am not Mrs. Hunt. Please make sure in the future that you get my name right. I hope you're not this careless with details when you write up your reports." She felt she'd gone too far as soon as the words had left her mouth, but she stood her ground, glaring up at him.

"May I speak now?"

"Go ahead," she said, folding her arms.

"As soon as you told me about Wendell and Mr. Hunt leaving the hotel together, I came out here to talk to Wendell's boss. I also called my partner and started a search for both of them. In addition, I've had backup dispatched to assist me, just in case there's trouble when Wendell returns."

"Assist you to do what?"

"Arrest Wendell Payne."

"You're going to arrest him?"

"As soon as I see him. I'm going to take him into custody, so we'll be able to question him thoroughly."

"And what about Mr. Hunt?"

"I'm hoping we'll find he's safe," Donovan said.

"Well ... if he's not safe, I'm holding you responsible. If you'd taken that man into custody in the first place . . ."

"We really didn't have any reason to before now," Donovan said. "But kidnapping, now that's something we can act on."

"You're also thinking Gil might have been kidnapped?"

"Yes I am. And we have you as our witness if it turns out that way."

Claire's anger slowly deflated. "You're going to arrest a man for kidnapping, based on my say-so?"

"You're the one who saw him push Mr. Hunt into a van."

"I never said 'pushed,'" she protested. "I said I saw them get into the van together."

"Well, we'll learn the truth soon enough," Donovan said. "We know where Wendell lives, and if he comes back to work, we'll have him."

"What if he never comes back?" she asked. "What if you can't find him or that maid?"

"Don't worry, Mrs. Duncan. We'll find them." And then with somewhat less confidence, he added, "The only question is, Will we find them soon enough?"

"Soon enough . . . for what?"

He reached out as if to give her a comforting pat but

then drew his hand back quickly. "Not to placate you, but just let us do our job. Things usually turn out okay when we're left alone to do what we've been trained to do."

At that moment, the front doors opened and two uniformed officers entered the lobby.

"Here are my boys," he said. "Excuse me."

While Donovan went to talk to the cops, Claire stood there with her arms still folded, wondering what she was supposed to do next. Had she just made a complete fool of herself in front of the detective? What if Gil had simply gone with Wendell for some reason that was none of her business? Was she way out of line here? And would he be angry with her because she had closed down his table? He was here to do business, after all.

No, that had been the right thing to do. His safety was much more important than selling a few more books. When she saw him and told him how concerned she had been, he'd understand. He'd probably have done the same thing if she'd left like that.

Now all she wanted to do was see him again.

CHAPTER 41

GIL AND WENDELL talked more during the ride back to the hotel.

"When you first started coming to Omaha a couple of years ago for your conventions," Wendell said, "Gracie wasn't working at the hotel yet. She only started there earlier this year. Man, when I first saw her, I knew she was the woman for me."

"If you don't mind my saying so, Wendell, she's a lovely woman, but she does seem to have a lot of issues."

"'Issues'? What do you mean?"

"There's a lot of bitterness inside her. Especially toward, uh, men. And about the way she feels she's been treated so unfairly since coming to this country."

"She had a real bad time of it in her own country," Wendell said. "She came here expecting things to be different . . . better, you know?"

"Ah, that old American dream—it gets 'em every time. Unfortunately, things don't always turn out the way people want them to."

"Well, I'm sure gonna try to make it turn out right for

her," Wendell said. "We just gotta get past this. She shouldn't be punished because she panicked and ran. That ain't right."

"Once the police hear her story, I'm sure they'll understand," Gil said, hoping he was right.

As they pulled into the hotel parking lot, they saw the police car out front.

"Oh Lord," Wendell said, "Now what?"

"Take it easy, Wendell. There's still a murder investigation going on, remember? They're probably just here to work on that."

Wendell swung the van into a parking spot. The men got out and walked to the front of the hotel. As they entered, Gil saw Detective Donovan in the lobby with two uniformed officers. When Donovan and the cops saw Gil and Wendell, they rushed them. Gil was pushed aside as the three men tackled Wendell to the ground and handcuffed him.

"Wendell Payne," Gil heard Donovan announce, "you're under arrest. Officer, read him his rights."

Donovan backed away, bumping into Gil as the two officers brought Wendell back to his feet and began reading to him from a printed card. Wendell looked totally confused, his eyes rolling about wildly.

"What the hell—" Gil began, but Donovan cut him off abruptly.

"Take it easy, Mr. Hunt. We'll need a statement from you, so don't go anywhere."

"Wait," Gil said loudly. "What are you—"

"I'm doing my job," Donovan said, putting his hand against Gil's chest. "Just stand back now."

"But you don't understand," Gil said, looking at Wendell. "We just—" He was brought up short by the look on Wendell's face, and the frantic way the big man was shaking his head. It was obvious Wendell didn't want Gil giving away the fact that they had just been to see Graciella.

"We're taking him in," Donovan said, "I'll come back to get your statement."

"What are you charging him with?" Gil asked. "Certainly not murder."

"No," Donovan said, "for now it's just kidnapping."

"What?" Gil asked, but he was speaking to no one as the three policemen dragged Wendell out to the squad car. Helplessly, Gil said aloud, "But who did he kidnap?"

Claire had decided to go into the bar. She needed a drink, and she could watch the lobby from there. She was sitting at one of the high bar tables when she heard the ruckus in the lobby. She saw the police push Gil aside and take Wendell down to the floor. She watched, as stunned as everyone else, then hurriedly left her seat and rushed out into the lobby. She reached Gil in time to hear him ask his question out loud.

"I'm afraid," she said, "that was all my fault."

Gil turned to face her, confused. "Claire, w—what just happened?"

She touched his arm. "I saw you leave with Wendell, and when Detective Donovan came by your table, I told him about it."

"And that was reason enough for them to arrest the man? Jesus," Gil said, putting his hand to his forehead. "What a mess."

"Where did you go? What were you doing with Wendell? I was so scared."

"Didn't you get my message?"

"Well, yes, but it hardly explained—"

"Who's watching my table?" he asked suddenly.

"I, uh, closed it," she said. "The man at the next table helped me cover it and—"

"Closed it?" he said, raising his voice.

"Well, I was worried about you! You call me, practically begging for help, and then disappear for the whole—"

"Okay," he said. "Okay. I'm sorry. Let's both calm down." He looked around and saw that, with Wendell having been taken away, he and Claire were now the center of attention.

"Let's got to the bar," he said, "and I'll tell you everything that happened."

She was very tempted just to walk out the front door and go home. "I don't know."

"Please?" he asked.

"Well... all right."

CHAPTER 42

THEY DECIDED NOT to go to the hotel bar, heading instead to the one across the street, where they had been together once before. They found a table and Gil went to the bar to get a beer for himself and a martini for Claire.

When he returned to the table, he set her drink in front of her, sat down, and took a healthy swig from his glass.

"Jesus," he said, shaking his head, "I still can't believe everything that's happened."

"Tell me about it." She waited for him to respond, and when he didn't, she said, "No, I mean it. Tell me about it now."

"Oh sorry. I guess I'm still kind of in shock. Okay, I went and met Donovan this morning. . . ."

He tried giving her the condensed version, but she wanted every tiny detail, and every conversation verbatim —especially when he got to the part about meeting Graciella.

When he was finished, she asked, "So, do you think she's guilty?"

"I don't know. She's got a gigantic chip on her shoulder,

and I have to say she's extremely bitchy to Wendell, who's only trying to help her."

"He's in love with her. Men in love are oblivious," Claire said, wondering why Gil didn't know that. "And being bitchy doesn't mean she's guilty of anything. What about Wendell?"

"What about him?"

"Do you think he could have killed Westerly?"

"Wendell? I don't know. What kind of a motive could he have had?"

"Maybe Westerly made a move on Graciella. You know, the exotic-looking maid? Maybe he found himself alone with her in the room and made a pass. Graciella told Wendell, or maybe he walked in on them?"

"Is making a pass at someone a reason to be murdered?"

"Believe me, I've known quite a few men who think it is. But maybe he didn't just make a pass; maybe he . . . attacked her, either verbally or physically."

"All I know is that Wendell doesn't belong in custody right now for kidnapping me."

"I am so sorry," she said. "I guess that's my fault."

"No, Donovan made the call, not you. And I'm partially to blame—for not leaving you a more coherent message."

"So, what do we do now?" she asked.

He stared across the table at her, wondering why she was even still there. He dared not ask, though. It might have brought her to her senses and sent her running home.

"I have to get back to the hotel," he said. "Detective Donovan is supposed to take me in to make a statement. I have to convince him to release Wendell."

"Just because he didn't kidnap you doesn't mean he didn't do something," she said. "And what about the maid? Graciella? Why didn't you tell Donovan about her?"

"Wendell didn't want me to," Gil said. "He made it very clear that I should keep quiet."

"Just because he loves her and wants to protect her, he certainly shouldn't expect you to feel the same way toward her. And he can't expect you to withhold anything from the police."

"No, but he trusts me. They both do."

"If she trusts you so much," Claire asked, "then why didn't she come back with you?"

"All right, so she doesn't trust me completely . . . yet. But he does."

"So how did you leave it with her?"

"I'm supposed to meet with her again tomorrow," he said. "She's going to decide whether or not to go to the police with me."

"But what about Wendell?" she asked. "Will she talk to you without him being there?"

"I'll just have to try to get him released first, then worry about that later."

"Will you still meet with her if he ends up in jail?" she asked.

"I guess the question will be, Will she still meet with me? Which brings me to another point."

He checked his watch. If he wasn't at the hotel when Donovan returned, the detective might put an APB out on him.

"What point?"

"I'll make this quick," he said. "I know I have no right to ask, but . . .".

"But what? Come on, spit it out." She smiled, trying to put him at ease. "You know you want to."

"I was thinking . . . maybe Graciella would be more

comfortable talking to a woman than to a man . . . than to me."

She sat back in her chair and stared at him, the look on her face a combination of surprise and incredulity.

"You want me to go with you to meet her?"

"The, uh, thought had crossed my mind."

"Why me?" she asked. "Why not one of your friends, another woman you know at the convention?"

"Because," he said, "believe it or not, I feel I already know you better than any other woman here."

CHAPTER 43

THE COUPLE WENT BACK to the hotel to wait for Donovan together. No one paid attention to them as they crossed the lobby to the bar. The place was quiet and things were back to normal.

They sat in a corner, drinking coffee and nibbling complimentary peanuts.

"What about your table?"

Gil shrugged. "Guess I'll have to write today off."

"You didn't do too badly."

"Really?"

She nodded. "I made some nice sales. None of the expensive stuff, but a lot of Westerly's books."

"That figures," he said. "Well, so maybe the day wasn't a total loss—businesswise, I mean."

"Is the dealers' room open tomorrow?"

"It's supposed to be, but who knows what I'll be doing then." When she didn't take the bait, he asked, "Have you decided to go with me to meet Graciella?"

"Still thinking about it. I'll let you know in the morning."

Gil looked up and saw Donovan enter the hotel. The detective stopped just inside and scanned the lobby.

"There he is. I better go."

She reached out and put her hand on his arm. "Meet me here for breakfast tomorrow?"

"Sure. How's nine?"

She nodded. "Be careful. I know you want to help Wendell, but you really don't know him. Running into someone once a year doesn't make you buddies. And you don't want to end up in jail yourself, do you?"

"The answer to that is a definite no," he said, then added to himself, Especially not now that I've found you. "You're really kind of amazing, you know?" he said aloud, surprising himself.

"Of course I know! You can't be this amazing and not know it, can you?" She hoped her attempt at humor hadn't come off sounding egotistical.

He returned her smile and then went out to the lobby to meet Donovan.

Gil was left to cool his heels in an interrogation room that was painted such a horrible drab green, he swore it almost smelled moldy. When Donovan finally entered, he was carrying two containers of coffee. He sat across from Gil and placed one in front of him.

"I've got sugar in my pocket, if you want it," he said. "Sorry, no milk."

"I take it black." Gil would have liked to ignore the offer, but he needed it. He removed the plastic lid and took a healthy sip. It was lukewarm and bitter, but at least it was coffee.

"I'm sorry you've had to wait so long, Mr. Hunt," Donovan said.

"I'm sure there was a reason."

"There's always a reason," the detective said. He had a folder with him and opened it now. Gil wondered if it was a prop. He looked around and didn't see a mirror on the wall. Of course, that didn't mean someone else wasn't listening.

"Mr. Hunt, I'd like you to tell me where you and Wendell Payne went today, and what you did."

"Where did he say we were?"

"I'd like to hear your version before I tell you that."

"Well, he didn't kidnap me; if you're still considering that theory, you're dead wrong."

"Glad to hear it," Donovan said. "That clears up some of this. If that's your statement, then we can't very well charge him with kidnapping."

"So you'll let him go, then?"

"No."

"Why not?"

"He's still a suspect in the murder of Robin Westerly."

"That's crazy," Gil said. "Why on earth would he want to kill him?"

"That's what we're trying to find out. Why would he, or his girlfriend, kill a mystery writer staying at a hotel where they both work?"

"Are they the only ones you're considering for the crime?"

"The investigation is still wide open," Donovan said. "There are a lot of suspects."

"A hotelful, Detective?" Gil asked.

"Well," Donovan said, "not quite that many. And maybe you can help me narrow it down even more."

CHAPTER 44

GIL DIDN'T HAVE A STORY.

He didn't want to tell Donovan where he and Wendell had gone. And he wasn't ready to turn Graciella over to the police. It would be better for her if she turned herself in.

"So?" Donovan asked.

"The track."

"What?"

"I had Wendell take me to the track."

"The racetrack?"

"Yes," Gil said. "Ak-Sar-Ben."

"I know the name of the track in town, Mr. Hunt," Donovan said sarcastically. "You mean to tell me you left your business, not to mention Mrs. Duncan, to go to the track?"

"That's right."

"That sounds—"

"Inconsiderate?" Gil suggested. "Irresponsible?"

"Yes. And it also sounds like a lie."

Gil sat back in his chair. "Why would I lie to a police detective?"

"That was going to be my next question."

"What did Wendell tell you?"

Donovan hesitated, then said, "He told me he took you to the track. You two must have worked this story out ahead of time."

"Why? Because somehow we knew you'd be waiting for him back at the hotel? And we also knew that as soon as we walked inside you were going to arrest him? We'd have to be mind readers, wouldn't we?"

Gil couldn't believe his luck. The lie had been all he could come up with, because it was all he and Wendell had ever had in common. Wendell coming up with the same story was more than he could have expected, but sometimes things just worked out.

"You obviously didn't stay for all the races," Donovan said, "so why did you have to go to the track at all?"

"I had a horse I liked."

"What horse?" Donovan asked, opening his notebook. "What race?"

"Fifth race," Gil said off the top of his head. "Horse number eight."

"What was the horse's name?"

"I don't know."

Donovan studied him. "So, you got a tip on a horse and you don't remember the name?"

"Who remembers horse's names?" Gil asked. "I got a tip to play number eight in the fifth race. I did it."

"And?"

"And it lost, so we came back."

"Why did Wendell stay with you?" Donovan asked. "Why didn't he drop you off and go back to work?"

"When I told him I was just going to play one horse in

one race because I had a tip, he decided to stay and put some money on it, too."

"And it lost."

"Yes." Gil shrugged. "Those're the breaks. Not every tip comes in."

"How did the horse run?" Donovan asked. "Where did it finish?"

"Look, Detective," Gil said, "all I know is that I played the horse to win and it didn't. Where it finished doesn't matter to me."

"How it ran doesn't matter to you? Did it go to the front? Come from behind? Was it blocked in the stretch?"

"I don't live here," Gil explained. "It's not like I'm going to follow the horse and play it again."

"Well, I do live here," Donovan said. "Maybe I'd like to follow it and play it."

"Be my guest. I'll get the name for you."

"No," Donovan said, "that's okay." He closed his notebook and put it away. "I'll check the results and find out the name for myself."

"Suit yourself."

Gil wondered how long he had before the lie fell apart. Would Donovan go to the track to check the results? Make a call? Or check the papers in the morning? He just wanted the lie to last long enough for him to meet with Graciella the next day and bring her here to the police station.

Donovan stood up.

"Are we done?" Gil asked.

"With the questions," the detective said. "There's no point in asking any more until I know whether or not you lied to me. I do need you to write down your statement, though—that you went to the track with Wendell Payne willingly and were not kidnapped."

"I can do that."

"I'll get you a pad," Donovan said; "then you'll have to wait while I have it typed up, so you can sign it."

"How long will that take?"

"Not long." Donovan left to get Gil a pad and pen.

Gil wondered if that would be long enough for Donovan to call the track. And he hoped that horse number eight had not won the fifth.

CHAPTER 45

WHILE GIL WAS at the police station, writing out his statement, Claire had gone home to calm down. She put on her favorite blue robe and curled up on the sofa with a cup of hot tea. Half an hour into an HBO movie, her son, Paul, came bursting into the room. "There you are!"

"Here I am," she said.

"You could have called, you know."

Claire laughed. "Hey, I thought that was my line."

"Come on, Mom, you know what I mean. It's all over the news. That writer guy getting killed. Why did you even have to go back there today? It's not safe!"

"Slow down. I was doing a favor for a friend."

"Gil Hunt, right?"

"Yes, I told you about him. And there probably isn't a safer place in town now, what with all the police around that hotel. Everyone's on their best behavior. It's like I have my own personal bodyguards."

"This isn't funny," he said. "How do you know who to trust? There's a psycho out there killing people—not like on TV, Mom, real people. You're doing everything you tell me not to," he complained, plopping down next to her. "You're trusting people too soon."

She put her cup down on the coffee table and hugged him. "Paul, sweetie, I know it's been tough on you since Dad and I split up. But you're a kid."

"I'm starting college in the fall, Mom."

"Honey, I don't need a father or a husband right now. I need a son—a seventeen-year-old son. I need him to be happy and have fun at his prom. I need him to inspire me with all kinds of great stories about college and girls. So please, stop worrying about your old mother."

"You're not old!"

"And you're sweet. And smart enough to flatter me into spending the next few days safe on this sofa instead of out having a life. Like you have."

"Fine. So you're okay?" He looked at her with those china blue eyes of his.

"Just tired."

"Then I'm going to the movies."

"Good. Have fun. Get outta here."

Paul started for the door. "Oh, old Mom, have you told your boyfriend about your bouncing baby boy yet?"

"Yes."

"Just checkin'."

She listened to his footsteps shuffling across the porch and down the steps. The engine in his old car finally turned over, and he drove off.

Would Paul like Gil? she wondered. Or would her son feel threatened by this man who was so different from his father? Gil Hunt was unlike anyone she or her son had ever known.

And now he wanted her to go with him and talk to Graciella. What if the woman had really killed Robin Westerly? That meant Gil was asking her to meet with a murderer. The prospect both thrilled and repulsed her. She shivered and drank more tea to chase the chill away.

But what if Graciella was innocent? And turning herself in to the police was the only way to prove it? And what if she would do that only if a woman showed up with Gil tomorrow? Then Claire would be helping an innocent woman avoid a murder rap.

Rap? She was starting to sound like some dame in one of those noir films. Claire found that funny and almost laughed out loud, but she felt silly.

She reached for the remote, searching for another movie —that was just starting. Maybe something on TCM. She found exactly what she wanted—*The Big Sleep*—and settled back into the cushions to watch it, thinking it wouldn't be such a bad thing to have Gil Hunt sitting on the other end of the sofa watching it, too.

Wendell Payne sat in the cell with his hands hanging down between his knees and his head bowed. He was worried about what Graciella would do if the police kept him in jail too long. They weren't going to let him talk to Mr. Hunt, so he could only hope that the man would be decent enough to meet with Gracie anyway, even without him. And he had to hope that Gracie wouldn't panic when she saw Gil Hunt drive up to the warehouse alone.

He wondered how much trouble he might have gotten Gil into by telling that lie about taking him to the track. It was the only story he could come up with. He was so nervous about his Gracie, he couldn't think straight.

Gil waited impatiently for his statement to be typed up. He hoped Donovan was not going to reenter the room and shove a results chart under his nose for that day's races at Ak-Sar-Ben. If Donovan found out about his lie while he was still in custody, he might decide to keep Gil in jail overnight. Gil had never been in jail before. In fact, he'd never even thought about being in jail before.

He wondered if he should just come clean and tell the truth. After all, why was he risking his neck for two people he hardly knew? This was not a hard-boiled mystery novel and he was far from being Mike Hammer.

Claire was getting ready for bed. After cleaning the kitchen, she turned off the lights and headed for the bathroom. The walls were in need of a fresh coat of paint and she'd had trouble deciding on a color. As she flicked on the switch, she thought maybe a soft apricot shade would be pretty. After brushing her teeth, she started to wash her face, and then it hit her—like an electrical charge zapped through her body. The memory of being in the hotel bathroom earlier that day, overhearing the cleaning women talking about Graciella. How could she have forgotten to tell Gil?

Donovan came in with Gil's statement and slid it across the table to him. "Read it over and make sure we didn't make any typos. Then sign it."

Donovan remained standing, arms crossed, while Gil read.

"It's fine."

He held out a pen to Gil. "Sign it, please."

Gil signed his name, then returned the pen and paper to Donovan.

"You're free to go, Mr. Hunt."

Gil was surprised. He had convinced himself he was going to have to tell the truth to avoid jail. As he stood up, his knees felt weak.

"What about Wendell?"

"We're keeping him, at least overnight," Donovan said. "There's a chance he still might tell us where the maid is— that is, unless you want to. If you do that, we might be able to cut him loose."

Gil hesitated. He knew Wendell would never tell, and he certainly wouldn't want Gil to, even if his silence meant the big man would have to stay in jail. Maybe he knew Wendell better than he thought after all.

"I can't help you, Detective. I have no idea where the woman is."

CHAPTER 46

"HOW COULD I have been so stupid?" Claire asked Gil the next morning.

"You're not stupid," he told her. "There's been a lot going on. A lot of strange things happening that would distract you."

She grinned. "Talk about your classic understatements."

They were sitting in the hotel restaurant, waiting for their breakfast. Claire wanted to confide in Gil as soon as they'd been seated, but the waitress wouldn't leave them alone until they'd ordered.

"Okay," Gil said, "so what did you want to tell me?"

They both leaned forward and Claire lowered her voice. Around them, other conventioneers were eating. Several mystery writers had already stopped by the table to say hello to Gil, all smiles and yellow badges. This was the first time she'd thought of his popularity as annoying.

As quickly as she could, Claire told him about the conversation she'd overheard in the ladies' room.

"A gun?"

"That's what they said."

"Are you sure they weren't just gossiping?"

"Well, of course they were gossiping," she said testily. "That's what women do in the ladies' room. But whether people believe it or not, gossip is usually grounded in some kind of truth."

"Okay, okay," Gil said, "so Graciella keeps a gun in her locker."

"And Robin Westerly was shot to death," she pointed out. "What does that tell you?"

"That Graciella may own a gun, but it doesn't prove she shot anyone."

"Don't you think this is something you should tell Donovan?"

He adjusted the napkin in his lap. "Under normal circumstances, yes.

"And these aren't normal circumstances?"

"No." He told her about his statement, which brought about another interrogation.

"You lied?" she asked. "Why would you lie?"

"I owe it to Wendell and Graciella—"

"You don't owe them getting yourself in trouble with the law!" she said, cutting him off. "God, are you *that* nice, or just terminally naive?"

"Claire, I told Graciella I'd give her a chance to turn herself in. So maybe she's not the sweetest person in the world—she does seem to have it in for men. And she owns a gun. But all of that doesn't make her a murderer. Not without evidence anyway. Once she's gone to Donovan, it won't matter that I lied."

"Let's hope not," she said. "Lying to the police is no small thing."

"I know that." He felt like a little boy being scolded.

Everything she'd said was right, and yet he still felt an obligation.

"I'll see her tonight. If she doesn't go to Donovan, I'll tell him everything. I just have to give her the chance."

"What if she's gone, Gil? Have you thought about what you're going to do if you go to meet her and she never shows up?"

"I'll have to take that chance."

"Ay," she said sitting back, covering her face with her hands.

At that moment, the waitress arrived with their breakfast and they had to wait for her to finish asking all her questions—"More coffee? Is everything all right? More water?"—before she went away.

"Look," he said, leaning forward again, "it may sound stupid—"

"I'll tell you something that sounds even more stupid," she said, dropping her hands. "I'm going with you tonight."

"You, don't have to do—"

"Yes, I do. Maybe I can talk her into going to the police and that will keep you out of trouble. Jesus, obviously you don't seem willing to help yourself, so I'm going to have to keep you out of jail."

Suddenly, he felt a smile coming, and he tried to hide it. "Is that a fact?"

"Yes, it is," she said. "We've only just gotten to know each other, but already I consider you one of my friends, and I can't have one of my friends going to jail because he's . . . he's . . ."

"Stupid?"

"No! Too nice for his own good."

"Thank you, Claire."

"Eat your breakfast," she snapped, hiding a smile of her own.

Neither of them knew it at that moment, but that was just the first of many times Claire would have to save Gil from himself.

"So what about Wendell?" she asked. "Are they going to let him out?

"I don't know. Donovan said they'd hold him overnight or until he told them where Graciella was, but at least they're not going to charge him with kidnapping."

"I still feel bad about that."

"Don't," he said. "You were worried about me. It just shows that you—" He stopped short.

"That I what?"

"Nothing. It was an honest mistake."

They both knew he was going to say something else, but each decided not to pursue it at that moment.

"What about your lie? Have you checked the results to see if that horse won?"

"No," he said, "I'm just hoping it didn't. And I don't want to look, because then I'll be waiting for the hammer to fall. I'll just have to hope I can stay out of Donovan's way until tonight."

Claire hesitated, then said, "You could come to my house."

"What?"

"I said—"

"I heard you. It's a nice idea, but no. That would get you too involved."

"And going with you tonight to meet with a possible murderer, that's not getting me 'too involved'?"

"Okay," he said, "but let's just not take all of this into your home. This is a big hotel and people are getting lost in it all the time. I'm sure I can avoid one police detective for one day."

They started to eat in silence and then Claire said, "I have a question."

"What is it?"

"If Graciella didn't kill Westerly, and Wendell didn't kill him, who did?"

"That's for Donovan to figure out," Gil said. "I'm just helping Graciella out. I'm not going to try to solve a murder."

"Funny," she said, poking at her food.

"What is?"

"Well," she said, "solving a murder . . . that sounds like it would be the fun part."

"Fun?"

"You know, asking questions, looking for clues . . . like Poirot."

"I'm afraid I don't have Poirot's little gray cells," Gil said. "Remember me? I'm just the nice, stupid man."

Claire knew that was her cue to argue, but instead of playing along with him, she stuck a wedge of melon into her mouth and kept quiet.

CHAPTER 47

THERE WERE STILL convention activities that Sunday until three o'clock in the afternoon. Gil had agreed to meet Graciella and Wendell at 6:00 P.M., and as he and Claire finished their breakfast, he tried to decide whether or not to open his table for business. If he did, he'd be an easy mark for Donovan should the detective come looking for him.

"You can't hide all day," Claire said to him as they left the restaurant. "*I'd* feel like the criminal if I had to hide all day."

"You're right," Gil said. "I'll open the table and if he comes, he comes. I don't think he can arrest me for lying to him. . . do you?"

"I'm no expert, but didn't you withhold evidence?"

"I don't know . . . maybe. Hell, what am I going to do? If I have to try avoiding him all day, I'm gonna really stress out."

"We could go downtown, to the Old Market, get away from here. Have you been there before?"

"No."

"This is your third trip to Omaha and you haven't been to the Old Market yet?"

"I usually stay in the hotel, or go to the track."

She put her hand on his arm to stop their progress toward the dealers' room. "If we go downtown, I can show you around, we can have lunch or an early dinner, and then we can go to meet Graciella from there. That way, you'll be away from the hotel and can't possibly run into Donovan. And maybe you might even have a good time."

"So . . . it would be like a date, then?"

She hesitated, then smiled. "Yes, it would be a date."

"Okay, then I accept."

They did not even stop by the dealers' room. Gil decided to leave the cover on his table and write the entire convention off as a bad business trip. As they headed for the lobby on the way to Claire's car, he spotted Spense coming toward him.

"Claire, I'll meet you at the car," he said. "I've got to talk to Spense."

"See you there. I just hope Donovan doesn't come walking in."

"You're right. I'll get out of the hall and find a corner."

She continued on and he moved to intercept Spense, already feeling like a criminal. Claire was right: Going downtown was the best plan.

"Spense . . ."

He managed to pull Spense into the alcove where the pay phones were.

"What's going on?" the convention organizer asked.

"I ran into your partner, Fleming, yesterday," Gil said. "He was frothing at the mouth because—"

"I know, I know. I talked to him. There were checks that

had to be written, and some decisions needed to be made. The guy's useless. I have to do everything."

From what Gil knew of Spense, he was a real control freak and would have set things up for anyone who was embroiled in helping him run the convention. He looked harried, and more disheveled than usual. As he stood there, he shifted his weight back and forth, constantly moving. If Gil hadn't known better, he would have thought the man was on something. And then he realized he didn't know better.

"Spense, are you okay?"

"No, I'm not. This whole convention has been a disaster from the start."

"With Westerly getting killed, you mean?"

Spense shook his head and then noticed a piece of lint on his sleeve and started picking at it. "Before that. Even before he got killed—the bastard—this convention was going to be a flop. I swear that this is the last one of these things I'm doing in Omaha, and next time I'm pickin' my guest of honor a lot more carefully."

"So you'll still do conventions?"

"I'm bidding on Bouchercon for Seattle in three years," Spense said. "I'm getting a big name for that one."

Bouchercon, named for Anthony Boucher, longtime mystery critic for the *New York Times* in the sixties, was the biggest mystery convention of the year. Held in a different city each year, the convention usually had around twelve hundred attendees. If Spense was this stressed-out about a local convention, Gil wondered if the man could handle the pressure of a Bouchercon.

"Well, I wish you luck with that. I just wanted to tell you about Fleming."

"Yeah, yeah . . . You headed for the dealers' room? I heard that's been a major disappointment, too."

"I'm skipping it today. Got a date."

"Sounds like a good idea. Wish I could run away from here." Spense turned to leave, then said, "And on top of everything else, I lost my pin."

"What pin?"

"My good-luck pin—you know, the one with the blue fedora on it. Either I lost it or the damn thing got stolen."

"Sorry—"

"That's probably why this whole thing went bad," Spense said.

Before Gil could comment again, Spense turned and rushed away. Gil figured if Spense continued doing conventions, he'd be a great candidate for an ulcer.

CHAPTER 48

GIL THOUGHT it was way past time for him to try for a kiss.

There had been a nice moment earlier, at breakfast, when it had occurred to him to lean over and softly touch Claire's lips with his. But there'd been too many people around—people he worked with, people he needed to maintain a certain level of professionalism with. And then there'd been the waitress, interrupting every five minutes.

He found walking through the Old Market with Claire —stopping into a pub for a beer, browsing in the antiquarian bookstore, and walking through one of the art galleries—so pleasurable that for a few hours he forgot all about Westerly, Donovan, and Graciella and started to look for an opening for that kiss.

The moment finally came when they were walking through a brick passageway between two restaurants. They stopped in a small alcove, dark except for a few rays of sunlight that filtered down through the thick ivy, to look at a fountain.

"I want to make a wish," Claire said. "Do you have any pennies?"

"I'm sure I do." He fished in his pockets, desperate to come up with a handful of pennies, because he already had formulated his plan of attack. Then he realized it didn't matter if he came up with pennies, nickels, or half-dollars, for he was going to give whatever he had to her to toss into the fountain.

As it turned out, he came up with several pennies and a nickel.

"Here you go," he said. He took her hand in his, pressed the change into her palm, then gently pulled her to him and kissed her.

It wasn't a peck, but it wasn't passionate, either. She didn't pull back; in fact, she leaned into him, so that it lasted long enough to be nice, but not too long to be embarrassing.

"What was that for?" she asked when they broke apart.

He smiled, still looking into her eyes. "For extra luck."

She smiled back, then turned toward the fountain, closed her eyes a second, opened them, and then tossed all but one of the coins into the water.

"There. Now you," she said, handing him the nickel.

"No." He grinned. "I just got my wish."

They went to Chez Chong for dinner around four o'clock. Most people had already had an early Sunday dinner, but those who hadn't eaten yet would be coming after five o'clock. This meant the couple had no problem finding a quiet, cozy table in the corner.

She had a beer with him, which he loved about her.

They had been talking the entire time, learning more about each other, but when the fortune cookies arrived, she grew quiet.

"What's wrong?"

"This has been nice, hasn't it?" she asked.

"It's been great."

"This is the kind of day I was hoping for when we first met. It's just perfect—except for . . ."

"Later tonight."

"Right. Do you know how to get to where Graciella is?" she asked.

"Yes. I only need to go someplace once to remember the route. It's a talent."

"It sure is," she said. "If I'm not driving, I don't pay any attention to directions at all."

He told her about the laundry service that dealt with the hotel, how Wendell knew the manager and had gotten use of the office.

"Will we be able to get in without Wendell there?"

"I hope so," he said.

"How's Graciella going to react when we arrive without him?"

"I just hope she doesn't panic."

Her eyes widened. "Let's just hope she doesn't have that gun with her."

"Good point."

They finished eating, then left the restaurant, strolling leisurely to the car. Impulsively, Gil took her hand and was pleased when she squeezed his in hers. By the time they reached the car, it was 5:00 P.M.

"Should we go now?" she asked. "We might get there too early. Maybe we should wait awhile."

He stopped walking. "I have a confession to make."

"What's that?"

He turned to face her. "I only know how to get to the warehouse from the hotel," he said sheepishly. "I'll have to drive back to the hotel and start from there. So I guess we better leave now."

She laughed and touched his face. "You're priceless."

"I sure hope the value keeps going up."

They didn't have to drive all the way back to the hotel, which made the possibility of running into Donovan very slim. By the time Gil got himself back to the intersection of Seventy-second Street and Dodge, things started looking familiar.

"What if the police released Wendell?" Claire asked.

"He'd probably go looking for me at the hotel, and when he didn't find me, he'd go to meet Graciella himself, hoping I'd show up."

"You never told me exactly why Wendell picked you to talk to her."

He shrugged. "I really don't know. I guess he thought I was a decent guy. Maybe he just doesn't know anyone else he can trust."

"So he trusted you. A guy he sees for a few days once a year?"

"I guess so," Gil said. "I can't explain it."

She studied him for a few moments, then stared out the windshield. "I think I can."

CHAPTER 49

IT WAS 5:50 when Gil pulled Claire's car into the parking lot of the Sparkling Clean Laundry Service.

"Do you see her car?" Claire asked.

"I don't even know what it looks like," Gil said. He studied the other vehicles in the lot but didn't know if they were the same ones that had been there the last time. Maybe the Ford Taurus, but he couldn't be sure.

They sat there for a few moments, waiting to see if another car would pull up.

"If she's inside, can she see us?"

"I think so."

"Then maybe we're making her nervous by just sitting here."

"You're right," he said. "We better go in. If she got here first, it'll be unlocked. Wait for me."

Gil got out of the car and rushed around to the other side to open Claire's door. If someone started shooting, he wanted to be able to protect her.

"Thank you," she said. As she got out, she realized how tense every muscle in her body was.

"Stay behind me," he said as they approached the building.

When they got to the entrance, they found it unlocked. Gil started for the office, taking the same path he had last time. Claire followed, never taking her eyes off the office door in front of them. But before they reached it, someone opened the door a crack.

"Stop there!" Graciella shouted. "Where's Wendell?"

Claire looked around, but the only cover she could see were pallets piled with bundles of sheets and towels. She wondered if they would stop a bullet.

"Graciella, listen," Gil said. "The police picked Wendell up yesterday when we got back to the hotel. They were waiting for us."

"How come they didn't pick you up, too?"

"They did," he explained. "They questioned me and let me go, but they're holding him."

"What for?"

"Well, they thought he had kidnapped me."

"That's crazy!"

"I explained everything to them, though."

"So why the hell they still got him, then?"

"Because he won't tell them where you are."

There was silence; then she said, "And you didn't tell them, either?"

"I don't know where you're staying, remember? I only know about this place."

"Who's that with you?"

"A friend of mine. Her name is Claire Duncan. She's attending the same convention I am."

"Why is she here?"

"I thought maybe you'd feel better talking to another woman," Gil said. "You can trust her. She wants to help."

"Yeah, you wanted to help me, too, and now Wendell's in jail."

"But I didn't put him there."

"Graciella," Claire said, "I was with Gil when he found you with Mr. Westerly."

"Oh," Graciella said, "you're that lady?"

"Yes. And Mr. Hunt's telling you the truth. It's not his fault Wendell's in jail."

"Then whose is it?"

Now they were stumped, wondering what they should tell her. They looked at each other.

Gil was about to speak, but just then Claire shouted, "It's your fault."

"Mine?"

"He refuses to cooperate with the police. They want to know where you are and he won't tell them."

Gil tensed, not knowing how Graciella would take what Claire had just said.

"He won't talk?"

"No," Claire said. "He loves you and thinks he's protecting you. Please, can we come in and talk? Maybe the three of us can figure something out."

They waited while Graciella made her mind up. Gil was also looking around for cover, formulating an emergency plan. He could push Claire behind the pallet on his left if—

"All right," Graciella said at last. "I guess you're okay. Both of you. You can come in."

She swung the door wide open but did not appear in the doorway. Obviously, she was going to wait for them inside.

"I'll go first," Gil said to Claire; "just stay behind me."

"If her gun is as big as those women said it was, it'll probably shoot a hole right through both of us."

"Thank you, Claire," Gil said. "That never occurred to me."

CHAPTER 50

CAUTIOUS, Gil entered the room, followed closely by Claire. Graciella was seated behind the desk, staring down at it morosely. Gil could not see her hands, so he didn't know if she was holding a gun or not.

"Graciella?" he said.

He and Claire stopped just inside the door. He wanted to be able to push Claire out of the room if he had to.

"I don't know what to do," she said, without looking up. "I don't have any money, Wendell's in jail, and . . . I'm all alone."

Claire brushed past Gil, and when he tried to stop her, she pushed his hands away.

"Graciella," she said, approaching the desk, "come with us. We'll go to Detective Donovan and you can turn yourself in. That will look much better for you than if you run and they have to hunt you down."

Graciella looked up at Claire with pain in her eyes. Her face was haggard. "It's not fair, is it?" she asked pitifully.

"What?"

"Life."

"No," Claire said, "it's not fair. I have a divorce behind me to prove it."

"I came up here with such dreams. I wanted to begin a brand-new life. But they don't let you. It's hard, very, very hard." She looked at Claire then. "I wasn't always poor. My grandfather was an important man in Mexico City. We had money, but my family lost all of it. My father . . . he killed himself, and my mother died only a year later in the gutter. So I came here to succeed. . . ."

"Gra—" Claire started forward to comfort the woman, but she stopped when Graciella brought the gun up from her lap. Quickly, Claire's heart leaped into her throat. Behind her, Gil experienced the same sensation.

"Do I look like a success?" Graciella asked both of them. "I clean toilets to make my money! And now because I was unlucky enough to be in the wrong place, I will be hounded."

"No one is going to hound you," Claire said. "Not if you give yourself up and tell your story."

Suddenly, Graciella smiled. "You're a nice lady. Very simpatico."

"Put the gun down, Graciella, please," Claire said.

Gil was impressed with Claire. He knew she had to be as terrified as he was, but he couldn't hear one quiver in her voice.

"You know," she said, "Wendell brought me this gun for protection, but sometimes I just feel like usin' it on myself."

"And what would that accomplish?" Claire asked. "Do you want them to win?"

"'Them'? You mean the police?"

"Yes," Claire said, "and everyone else who has treated

you unfairly. Show them you can succeed in spite of everything you've been through."

"But I can't."

Then Claire surprised Gil by asking Graciella the question he had never thought to ask her himself: "Did you kill Mr. Westerly?"

"No, I did not," Graciella said, turning the gun over in her hands. It was a big black automatic—Gil and Claire knew at least that much from watching cop shows. A man's gun, Gil thought.

"Gracie," Gil said, taking a couple of tentative steps forward, "why not give me the gun and then we can all figure out what to do next? You don't want to take the chance of someone getting hurt, do you?"

Graciella switched her gaze from Claire to Gil. Her grip on the gun loosened, causing it to drop slightly toward her lap.

"I don't want to hurt nobody. But I don't want to go to jail, neither."

"If you're innocent, it will come out," Gil said. He moved closer still, until he was even with Claire. This close, he could feel the tension in her body.

"Come on, Gracie," Gil said, "give it to me."

He got close enough to be able to reach across the desk and accept the gun, if she was willing to give it up, when all hell broke loose.

Suddenly, the room was filled with uniformed police officers as they came charging through the doorway, guns drawn. Gil and Claire were shoved roughly aside.

"Drop it! Drop it!"

"Hands up!

"Don't move!"

Graciella was yanked out of her chair and the gun torn from her hands before she could do anything. They got her down on the ground the same way they'd taken Wendell down the day before. Then they cuffed her. When that was done, Donovan came walking in.

"Graciella Sanchez, you're under arrest," Donovan said. "Take her out."

The cops pulled her up off the floor and she glared venomously at both Gil and Claire.

"You told me to trust you, and you brought the police!" she spat. *"Cabron! Puta!* I'll make you regret what you've done to me. I'll get both of you! No matter what I have to do, I'll—"

"Get her out of here!" Donovan shouted.

As they dragged her from the room, still shouting epithets in Spanish, Gil faced Donovan.

"You son of a bitch, you followed me?"

"We've had you under surveillance all day, Mr. Hunt. By the way, real smooth move by the fountain."

"You bastard—" Claire began, but Donovan cut her off.

"Don't make me arrest the two of you," he said, "because believe me, I can come up with some charges."

"She didn't kill anyone," Claire said.

"That's for a court to decide, not me," Donovan told her. "My job is to bring her in."

"Jesus," Gil said to nobody in particular, "she thinks we gave her up. . . ."

"What does it matter what she thinks?" Donovan asked. "Or what anybody thinks? You folks are through with this. Right here and right now! Go home and forget about it. Read your books. Leave solving the mysteries to the professionals."

Gil and Claire, speechless in their anger and frustration, glared at Donovan as he started toward the door.

At the door, the detective turned and said, "Oh, and Gil? You should have played that horse, man. Number Eight horse in the fifth? It won and paid sixty-eight dollars!"

CHAPTER 51

IF THAT GOOD-FOR-NOTHIN' wasn't there when she got out, there'd be hell to pay. But she couldn't piss him off until after. Then she'd punch it into his thick head, if she had to, show him just how much better off he'd be if he realized she didn't need anything from him except to drive her out there. And if she had the money, she wouldn't even need him for that.

She didn't need anyone—especially not no man. She could take care of herself. There were a couple of bitches and one guard in particular who were carrying around the scars to prove it.

Poor sap, writing all those damn letters. Still goin' on and on about love and that kind of bullshit. The only thing interesting at all in any of them were the newspaper clippings he'd stuck inside. Like the one announcing that couple was getting married. What a cheesy-ass picture, with all them teeth and smiles. It made her wanna puke. And then the announcement that they were living in St. Louis. Her with that fancy job on TV and him and all his bookstore shit.

Oh, yeah, there was one letter she'd kept. Wendell'd told

her about a conversation he'd had with one of his brain-dead friends, the guy who worked out at that resort—the one where those Hunts were going to be staying.

So, after they saw to it that she got locked up—good and tight—they went off and got rich and famous. Good for them. That'd make the payoff even better. Maybe they'd have some of that money stashed in their fancy room. And maybe she'd just take it when she was done.

CHAPTER 52

GIL STOPPED TALKING and poured himself another cup of coffee.

"Wow!" Tucker said.

"I never imagined . . . I had no idea you two went through something like that," Reagan said.

The coffee had gone cold and Gil put his cup down abruptly.

"I can make some more," Claire offered, but he waved her away.

"No, it's fine," he said. "I'm dry after all that talking. I'll just have some water."

"Do you mind a few questions?" Reagan asked.

"You must be tired of the sound of my voice. Claire can take over now."

"So what happened to Graciella?" Reagan asked.

Claire handed Gil a glass of water and then sat down next to him. "She went to prison. We don't know all the details, but apparently her lawyer plea-bargained and the charge was reduced to manslaughter."

"In jail for how long?" Tucker asked.

"We're not sure."

"But . . . do you think she did it?"

Claire looked at Gil, who simply shrugged.

"To this day," Claire said, "we don't think they had enough evidence to prove she did anything."

"She had a gun," Reagan pointed out.

"But it wasn't the same caliber as the one that killed Westerly," Claire replied.

"She was going to run," Tucker said.

"Out of panic."

"And what about Wendell?" Tucker asked.

"Still in Omaha," Gil said. "He kept his job."

"Do you suppose he and Graciella stayed in touch?" Reagan asked.

"We don't know," Claire said.

"We're talking about two love stories here," Reagan commented, "yours and theirs."

"I thought we were talking about murder," Gil said.

"That, too, but Reagan's a romantic. She would zero in on the romantic part of any story," Tucker said.

Reagan playfully punched her husband in the arm but didn't deny the accusation.

"I get the feeling you two think she was innocent," Reagan said.

"It doesn't matter what we think," Gil said. "She ended up in prison anyway."

Claire leaned over and rubbed Gil's back.

Reagan thought a moment and then asked Gil, "Do you feel guilty?"

"Of course I do. That damn cop used me, followed me—"

"Followed *us*," Claire interjected.

"—and as a result, Graciella ended up in jail. I tried

talking to Wendell, but he wouldn't have anything to do with me. And that bastard Donovan never returned one of my calls."

"Graciella wouldn't see us, either," Claire said.

"So she must still blame you, even after all these years," Reagan said. "That's so sad, for you and for her."

They all fell silent for a few moments and it became obvious that the evening had finally come to an end.

"Well," Tucker said, "it's getting late."

The four of them stood, and Gil and Claire walked their guests to the door.

During a hug good-bye, Reagan said to Gil, "It wasn't your fault, you know. How could you have possibly known you were being followed?"

"He couldn't," Claire said, putting her arms around her husband. "Neither of us could."

Tucker hugged Claire, and Reagan said, "Thank you two for sharing your story with us. And don't worry, I promise not to use one word of it in my book."

After their guests had left, Gil offered to help Claire clear away the mess, but she shooed him out to the deck, where he could enjoy the night air. When she came out, he was leaning on the railing, staring out at the water. She had two glasses of wine with her and handed him one.

"A nightcap," she said.

"Thanks."

She stood next to him, enjoying the absolute stillness that surrounded them. "Good memories connected to bad ones, huh?"

"Uh-huh."

"But I think the good far outweigh the bad, don't you?" she asked.

He turned to look at her, then smiled and snaked an

arm around her waist. "Definitely, because the good means I got to spend the past seven years married to you."

"And there are still many more to come."

"I'll drink to that."

They touched glasses, then went inside to have their own private anniversary celebration.

CHAPTER 53

CLAIRE WAS the first to wake up the next morning. She got out of bed without Gil—not a very hard thing to do, since he always slept soundly—pulled on her robe, slid into her slippers, and padded out to the kitchen. Pushing aside the curtains covering the large windows, she was again struck by the beauty of Big Cedar. Colors seemed so much more vivid in the Ozarks. Watching three squirrels dash through a pile of leaves, she couldn't resist sliding the patio door open and sitting outside a moment before fixing breakfast.

There were never moments like this back in St. Louis. Everything was so pumped up in the city: traffic, music, people. She was thinking how easily she could get used to this place, especially as she remembered the day they had moved into their condo in the city.

The balcony had seemed such a nice feature. And that first morning, after all the boxes were unpacked, she'd gotten up and gone outside, trying on her new surroundings for size. But then the construction workers spotted her up there and her neighbors tried carrying on a conversation from one floor overhead. That first outing became the last.

After twenty minutes to herself, Claire couldn't ignore the grumbling coming from her stomach and went inside to put on a pot of coffee for Gil and brew a cup of tea for herself. If she remembered correctly, there should be some bread for toast.

At home, she was always the first one to leave in the morning. As a treat, she thought she'd pamper Gil and take him his coffee today. As she started to leave the kitchen and enter the living room, she was so startled that she cried out and dropped the mug, which struck the kitchen floor and shattered.

"Stand very still," the woman said, pointing the gun at Claire's head.

Gil heard the commotion and shot out of bed. No matter how soundly he always slept, if someone—his kids when he was younger, and now Claire—shouted or called out, he woke immediately. He didn't know what was going on, but he hit the floor running and didn't stop until he got to the living room. When he saw Graciella Sanchez standing there with a gun, he jerked to a stop.

At least he thought it was Graciella. The woman glaring at him was a much harder-looking version of the woman he'd last seen all those years ago in Omaha. Her hair was chopped short, her cheekbones seemed much more pronounced, and her eyes were dull.

"Graciella?" he said.

"Ah, *bueno,* you remember me, Mr. Hunt. I am very flattered."

Gil was acutely aware of the fact that her gun was not

pointed at him, but at Claire, who was standing in the doorway to the kitchen, shoulders hunched. Her body language told him she was afraid, but her eyes were defiant.

"Wha—what the hell—" Gil stammered, not yet fully awake.

"I'll give you a moment to get your bearings. So sorry to have spoiled your beauty sleep." Graciella gestured with the gun. "This is probably a great shock."

"Yes. Yes, it is."

"I frightened you, Mrs. Hunt?"

"Yes."

"Good. I wanted you to know how it feels to be help-less," she said. "When the police took me away, I told you that you would regret what you did to me. And I meant it."

Gil noticed she held the gun with much more confi-dence than she had years ago.

"Graciella, listen—"

"There will be time to talk later," she said, cutting him off. "Mr. Hunt, please go now and unlock the front door. Your pretty wife wasn't so kind as to open it for me like she did the other one."

"You were outside on the deck? Waiting to get in?" Claire asked, even more frightened.

"I thought you'd never go back inside." Graciella snick-ered. "But I could have gotten in without your help. I've learned a lot of important things in prison. A great many. Now, please, the front door."

"Graciella, take that gun off my wife. Point it at me, if it makes you feel safer," Gil said.

"No, no," the woman said. "I'm pointing it exactly where I want to. Now don't make me tell you again. Open the door!"

Gil had to cross between Graciella and Claire. Briefly,

he considered rushing her and trying to wrestle the gun away, but that would force the issue and someone would definitely get hurt. He reached the front door and opened it.

"Wendell? What are you doing here?"

Before Wendell could reply, Graciella shouted, "Come back to the center of the room. Wendell, *mi vida,* close the door and be sure to lock it behind you."

Gil looked at Wendell and the big man shrugged helplessly. He didn't have a gun, and it seemed that somehow he had grown even larger over the years. Studying Wendell, Gil knew he had no chance of overpowering him. He turned and walked back to the living room, his mind racing, looking for a way out.

CHAPTER 54

"*GET OVER* THERE and stand by your wife," Graciella ordered. Gil could feel her seething anger rippling toward him across the room.

Claire had moved and now stood in the living room, her back to the open sliding doors leading to the deck.

"I suppose you're wondering why we came to visit you so unexpectedly?" she asked them.

"I think I can guess," Gil said. "Graciella—"

"You will not speak to me, Mr. Hunt!" she snapped. "I have spent eight years waiting for this moment, planning how I would pay you both back for what you did to me."

"But we didn't do anything," Claire said. "We had no idea the police were following us that day."

"Ah, good," Graciella said, "then you remember what you did."

"Neither one of us has been able to forget that day, Grace," Gil said.

"But you went on with your lives, no? You got married. You know, I looked for my wedding invitation, but it never came." She grinned, her hand still holding the gun to

Claire's head. "No matter, 'cause I didn't have a thing to wear."

"We tried to see you after you were arrested," Claire said.

"We called Detective Donovan, but he wouldn't talk to us," Gil added.

Donovan had turned out to be a real piece of work. He had used Gil, followed him that last day, and then, after taking Graciella in, dropped off the face of the earth. All the news they could get came from newspapers and TV reports. Even Wendell wouldn't have anything to do with them.

"We heard your lawyer had to plea-bargain the charge down to manslaughter."

"He told me," she said, "that they would not convict me if I said it was an accident. Accident, my ass. I told that man over and over that I never killed no one. But he wouldn't listen to me—none of them would. I didn't know what to do, so I agreed—and those fuckers sent me away for ten years."

"But, you're out—"

"Eight years," she said, "good behavior. Once I learned how to play the game in prison, I became very well behaved. I also became very well educated. And look at me now," she said with pride. "I am not meek, I am not frightened, and I do not depend on men. I make my own decisions."

"Like this one?" Gil asked. "Coming here, threatening us with a gun? This is what you decided?"

"This is what I have planned for years," she said. "I've seen it in my mind over and over again. I'm not here just to threaten you. Don't you get it? I'm here to kill the two of you miserable liars."

"Wendell," Gil said, "you can't be going along with this."

"Gracie," Wendell said, "you can't just . . . shoot them in cold blood. This isn't what we talked about doin'."

"'We'? This is what I need to do, Wendell," she said, "and that's all that matters."

"But—"

"Shut up!"

Wendell shrank back from her biting tone, taking on the attitude of a whipped dog. Gil had known back in Omaha that Graciella was the dominant personality in their relationship, but now that she had obviously changed, she was not just dominant but overpowering, too. No, he and Claire weren't going to be getting any help from Wendell.

Gil got a cold feeling in the pit of his stomach as he thought of Graciella hurting Claire, and standing next to him, Claire was having the same thoughts. Like people in love are wont to do in a crisis, they were thinking only of each other, not themselves.

Gil looked at Graciella and Wendell, remembering how Reagan had commented the night before that their story had actually been two love stories. It was obvious now one of those stories would not have a happy ending. If Graciella had ever loved Wendell, it was glaringly obvious that she no longer did. She only needed him to help get her revenge. Maybe, just maybe, Gil could get this across to Wendell. It was the only thing he could think to do, unless Claire chimed in with a better idea.

"Wendell," Gil said, "man, this is not right and you know it. We tried helping you, but we were victimized by Donovan and the police just like—"

"Me!" Graciella screamed. A vein along her neck bulged and her face reddened. "How dare you compare your discomfort to my suffering! Did you and your precious wife go to jail? Did you spend night after night hoping for a miracle, praying that somehow the truth would show itself and you'd get to go home?" She looked at Claire. "Have you changed as much as I have in the past eight years, Mrs. Hunt? Have you been forced to become less than human?"

"Grac—" Claire began.

"No." For the first time, her grip wavered and the gun moved back and forth between Gil and Claire. "No more words. The only decision I have to make now is which of you I will shoot first."

"Me," Gil said, mentally trying to send Claire a message to run when Graciella turned the gun on him.

"Wendell," Claire said, her eyes pleading with the big man, "you can't let her do this. Please." She didn't want to give either one of them the satisfaction of seeing her cry, but she couldn't hold back a sob caught in her throat. "You can't let her hurt Gil; he was only kind to you."

Gil looked at Wendell, who stood with his shoulders slumped, a mournful look on his face.

"Gracie, baby . . ."

"I told you to shut up, Wendell."

"I can't. I've done everything you asked me to. I waited for you. I loved you all these years. I kept track of Mr. and Mrs. Hunt here. I found out where they'd be on the day you got out, and then I picked you up and brought you here to talk to them. That's what you said, that you wanted to talk to them. But I didn't bring you here to kill them. No way."

"Then you're stupider than I told all my friends you were," Graciella said. "What did you really think I wanted to do? Slap their little pasty wrists and say, 'Shame on you bad people for sending me to prison'? Do you think an apology is good enough?"

"Gracie, listen—"

"You're stupid and useless, Wendell."

Claire saw Wendell flinch, as if his precious Gracie had physically struck him.

"When I finish with them, I'm finished with you."

"But you'll be on the run," Wendell said, obviously still concerned with her welfare.

"I've made my plans, plans that do not include you."

Wendell's chin fell onto his chest, and both Gil and Claire felt that their last chance—their only chance—had passed.

"Gracie—" Gil said.

"Basta! Enough! It's time to get this done, and since you were the main offender, Mr. Hunt, your wife will feel the first bullet."

"No!" Gil shouted, leaping in front of Claire.

"Gracie, no!" Wendell yelled, and jumped for Graciella.

The big man slammed into the woman, knocking her to the floor. She maintained her hold on the automatic in her hand and, cursing Wendell out, struck at him with it.

Gil turned quickly, taking advantage of the moment. He tackled Claire and pulled her out onto the deck, where they struck the rail together and went over.

CHAPTER 55

THE DROP onto the dirt forced air from Gil's lungs, but he turned

quickly to look for Claire and see if she was all right.

"Gil!" she called.

They grabbed each other. Gil had landed hard on his shoulder and now felt something warm running down his face.

"You're bleeding," she said, touching his head.

"How are you?" he managed to croak.

"I banged my hip and elbow, but I'm okay."

"Come on," he urged. "We have to run."

"But—" Claire began, only to be cut off by a horrible scream. From the sound of it, Graciella's rage was being released not only at the couple but at Wendell, as well.

"Come on!" He dragged her to her feet and they started running.

Claire was still in her robe and slippers, which made it difficult to run over the rocky terrain, but Gil was in worse shape. Dressed only in lightweight pajamas, his feet were bare. The rocks had already cut into his soles several times.

But they kept running.

Graciella came out onto the deck and fired several shots at them.

They had no idea where they were running to, and Gil finally halted their progress to take stock. They could hear boats out on Table Rock Lake but couldn't see anyone from where they hid.

"Listen, there are people not far from here. We have to make it to the main lodge or the marina," he said.

"Gil, she's crazy." Graciella was still screaming as she tried to find them. "Maybe she'll run out of bullets."

"I doubt it. That's an automatic she's got. It could have as many as eighteen bullets in it. And she might have another clip with her."

He looked down then and saw his bloody footprints, and he suddenly became aware that in spite of the pain, his condition could work to their advantage.

"Let's split up," he said.

"What?" Are you crazy?"

"One of us will make it and get help. The trails are marked well. Just keep heading for the lodge."

Claire looked at the ground and realized what he was planning. "Jesus, your poor feet. You're leaving a trail; she'll be able to follow you."

"Right, and if we're together, she'll be following both of us. You have to—"

"Oh no," she said, "you're not getting rid of me, not after only seven years. We're staying together."

"Claire, honey—"

"Together!" she said, grabbing his arm. "Now let's go. She's getting closer."

They started running again. All the while, Graciella screamed their names and fired shots into the trees around them. Gil feared for Wendell's safety as well as their own. The big man had saved their lives, but at what price?

It was becoming increasingly difficult for Gil to keep going with his feet so badly cut. "Wait, wait," he finally said.

"What's wrong?"

"Sweetie, I just can't keep up. You have to go on without me."

"Here, take my slippers," Claire said desperately.

"They won't fit. And then we'll both be banged up."

"Take off your shirt," she said. "We'll tear it and wrap your feet."

He took her tear-stained face in his hands and thought she had never looked more beautiful. "Please, just go get help."

"I can't . . . I just can't. Gil, don't ask me to leave—"

Then they heard a scream.

And a single shot.

Then silence.

They waited, listening for her crazed screaming to start up again. But it didn't.

"What happened?" Claire asked.

"I don't know."

They continued waiting.

"Do you think she stopped?"

"She must have," he replied, "but why?"

They were both crouched down, and now they sat on the ground. They were sweaty, grimy, and bloody, but grateful for the chance to catch their breath.

And then another scream, but this one anguished, and it came from a man.

CHAPTER 56

IN THE ENSUING SILENCE, they took time to tear Gil's pajama top into strips and wrap his feet.

"Can you walk?" Claire asked.

"I'll have to. Try to find me something to use, a big branch—"

"Just lean on me," she said.

They started making their way back. The closer they got to the cabin, the louder the sound of sobbing became.

"I wonder what happened," Claire said. "Graciella wouldn't just stop chasing us."

"Maybe we're crazy to be going back the way we came."

But they continued, not knowing where else to go, and finally the sobbing became loud enough for them to pinpoint its origin. When they reached the source, they found Wendell at the base of a steep hill, sitting on the ground, holding Graciella in his arms.

"Oh God," Claire said.

They staggered down the hill, coming to a standstill, then dropping to the ground themselves.

Graciella was covered in blood. The gun lay next to her.

"Oh my God, Wendell. What happened?" Gil asked.

"My poor baby. My sweet, sweet girl," the big man said over and over as he rocked her.

"I'll go call for a doctor," Claire said. She was turning to run back to the cabin, when Wendell spoke.

"No need. She's gone."

"How?" they asked in unison.

"She came to the top of this hill. I was chasin' her, shoutin' for her to stop. She didn't figure on it bein' so steep, and she fell."

"And the gun went off?" Gil asked. "Is that what happened, Wendell?"

The man just shook his head.

"Claire," Gil said, keeping his voice low, "get the gun."

Warily, Claire moved closer to Wendell and Graciella, reaching for the weapon. But she needn't have been so careful. Wendell was oblivious to everything around him except for the dead woman in his arms. Claire grabbed the gun and crawled back to Gil.

They sat with Wendell for several minutes. He fell silent after a while. The three of them were so quiet, they could hear the birds in the trees and horses far off in the stables.

"Wendell," Gil said, but the big man did not look up. "Wendell, did she do it? Did she kill Robin Westerly?"

Finally, he looked up at them, his face streaked with tears and dirt. Just as she had been chasing them, he had obviously been running after her. There was a long gash across his bald head, where she must have struck him with the gun.

"No," he said. "She didn't kill him."

Despite the fact that they both had been put through hell that morning, they felt sorry for him . . . and for

Graciella. Donovan had screwed her over by taking the easy way out. He had used Gil and Claire as the bait to put her under arrest. She'd taken the advice of her lawyer and ended up in jail. And because of her past, she was unable to return the love of the only person who treated her well.

"Wendell," Gil said, "I'm sorry."

With his big hand, Wendell reached into one of Graciella's pockets, removed something, and tossed it to Gil. It struck Gil in the chest, then fell into his lap. It was a pin in the shape of a blue fedora.

"What—" Gil said.

"She found that in the dead man's room. She said she picked it up off the floor just before you came in."

"On the floor?" Gil asked. He turned it over in his hand and then brought the pin closer to examine it.

"What is it?" Claire asked.

"This pin was Spense's lucky piece."

"Spense? Then how did it end up on Robin Westerly's floor?"

Gil clenched it in his fist. "He told me he lost it."

"But if he lost it in Westerly's room—"

"Jesus," Gil said, "Spense must have killed him."

Claire couldn't believe what she was hearing. "But why?"

"They argued," Wendell said.

They both looked at him. Gil asked, "When?"

"That first night at the hotel. I drove them to dinner, and on the way back they argued about whose fault it was that more people weren't cornin' to their convention. Mr. Westerly said it was the other man's fault because he didn't know what the hell he was doin'. The other man said that Mr. Westerly wasn't important or famous enough to make people want to come."

"That would be enough to make Spense kill Westerly?" Claire asked.

"Mr. Westerly said he knew about something in the other man's past," Wendell said. "Something that would keep him from putting on another convention ever again."

"Spense told me about a problem he'd had with money at a past job. And he was hoping to put on a Bouchercon in Seattle."

"He could have made a lot of money doing that," she said. "I mean, with the size that Bouchercon has become, even back then he could have made some money."

"It isn't like people haven't been accused of stealing in the past," Gil said. "Another thing, Spense seemed real . . . on edge that weekend."

"So you think he was . . . unstable enough to kill his guest of honor? Sabotaging his own convention?"

"Why not?" Gil said. "If it meant saving his chance for a big payday at a huge convention? Too bad for him he never had the chance to do it."

"Why?"

"Don't you remember? About two years after that Omaha convention, he committed suicide. Shot himself in the head, right in his own kitchen."

Her eyes widened. "I completely forgot."

"I've worried about that for years," Wendell said. "Worried and prayed that it wasn't my fault."

They looked over at him again.

"How could that have been your fault?"

"I was . . . angry about Gracie bein' in jail, and I couldn't do nuthin' to get her out. I didn't have money for another lawyer, for an appeal. So I started . . . callin' him. Got his name and address from the hotel."

"You called him? Why would you do that?" Claire asked.

Wendell shrugged his big round shoulders. "Just kept callin', botherin' him all times of the day and night, tellin' him I knew he was the killer."

"But you didn't know that," Gil said. "Why would you do such a thing to him?"

"I knew there was a better chance he was guilty than my Gracie."

"So why didn't you take the fedora pin to the police?" Claire asked. "Wouldn't it have been better to give them evidence than to stalk a man?"

"I tried tellin' Detective Donovan, but he wouldn't hear nuthin' I had to say. He said the case was closed an' I should leave him alone."

They fell into silence again. Wendell continued rocking Graciella while Gil and Claire tried to make sense of everything they'd just heard.

"Claire, why don't you go back and call for help?"

"All right." She touched his shoulder. "Don't try to move, or your feet will start bleeding again."

"We'll wait here."

She nodded, stood up, and started back up the steep hill.

Wendell reached down and stroked Graciella's face. "She really wasn't a bad person, Mr. Hunt."

Gil had known her back then, and he'd experienced the person she'd become after prison. He didn't think he could ever think of her as a "good" person in either incarnation. But what he said was, "I'm sure she wasn't, Wendell."

EPILOGUE

ST. Louis, One Year Later

Gil came out on the balcony of their condo, where Claire was staring down at Brentwood Boulevard.

"Happy anniversary," he said, handing her a cup of tea.

She accepted the cup, kissed him, and went back to leaning on the railing.

"What are you thinking about?" he asked.

"Same thing I always think about this time of year."

"Conventions in Omaha."

"But this anniversary, we've got Big Cedar, as well as Wendell and Graciella, to add to the list."

"I guess you were right about not going back there to celebrate this year," he said, standing next to her.

"Too many memories." Then she looked down and said, "Your poor feet."

It had taken weeks for the soles of his feet to heal once they had returned to St. Louis. And the scratches and bruises they each had suffered took just as long.

"Our life has become like that movie, *Same Time, Next Year,*" she said. "Only instead of meeting at the same romantic place every year, we're haunted by the same murder."

"We're never going to be free of the memories."

"You know, on one hand, I felt so sorry for Graciella," she said, "but on the other hand, I hated her. She was a royal bitch who got everything she deserved—well, except for being sent to prison."

"Yeah, I guess the only good thing you can say about her is that she wasn't a murderer."

"No one would have ever known that if it wasn't for you," Claire said. "And poor Wendell... he saved our lives, but at what cost?"

"I think he came out all right," Gil said, putting his arm around her shoulder. "Look, why don't we just concentrate on our date tonight to celebrate eight years of marriage?"

She leaned her head against his shoulder. "You're right. Too bad we both have to work, or we could spend the whole day together." Claire was due to be on the air in two hours. Gil had not been able to find anyone to watch his bookstore, so he had to go in to unpack several shipments he was expecting.

"That's okay," he said. "We'll meet back here tonight, get all dressed up, and go out on the town."

"I can hardly wait." She leaned forward and kissed him. "But now I've got to go dress and get out of here."

She had to be at the station by 9:00 A.M., while he didn't have to be at the bookstore until 11:00.

"Okay, I'm gonna stay out here awhile longer."

She touched his cheek, then his shoulder, and went inside. He stared down at the street, alone with his thoughts. . . .

Upon their return to St. Louis a year ago, Gil had put in a call to Detective Jason Holliday of the St. Louis Police Department. After he explained the situation, Holliday remained silent for a few moments before speaking.

"This sounds like a lot of hassle. Why would I want to do what you're asking?"

"Because I happen to know you hate unsolved crimes," Gil said, "especially murders. And you really hate seeing the wrong person go down for a murder. This is a case of both."

Another hesitation, and then Holliday said, "All right, I'll make some calls."

Several days later, Holliday called Gil and they arranged to meet at his bookstore on Delmar.

When Holliday arrived, Gil asked, "Will you let me buy you lunch? We can go to Fitz's or Blueberry Hill . . ."

"Right here is fine for me," Holliday said.

"How about a cup of coffee, then?"

"Sure."

Gil went to the front door, locked it, and flipped the OPEN sign to the sign that said BACK SOON.

"Follow me."

He took Holliday to the back of the store, where he had a coffeemaker going. He got two mugs, poured them full, and handed the detective one.

"You remembered I take it black. I'm impressed, Mr. Hunt."

"No problem."

They sat down, Gil in an overstuffed chair he'd placed

back there for when he wanted to relax, and Holliday on a metal folding chair. The detective took out his notebook and opened it.

"It wasn't easy, but I talked to a detective in Seattle and to your buddy Donovan in Omaha. He's a real asshole, by the way."

"I know."

"He's also a lieutenant now," Holliday said. "Seems his rise to the top began with the arrest of Graciella Sanchez, which means he's not a happy camper right now, and neither are his superiors."

"You mean—"

"Yep," Holliday said. "We were able to check the bullet that killed Dave Spenser against the bullet that killed the writer Robin Westerly."

"And?"

"They matched perfectly," Holliday said. "A check of Spenser's background revealed problems with several employers. He was involved with missing funds, and his erratic behavior caused a great many headaches. Your friend pissed off a lot of people."

"He wasn't my friend," Gil said. "I mean, not really. We'd see each other once or twice a year at conventions. We were just acquaintances, really. And how can you tell someone's state of mind from that?"

"Apparently, you can't," Holliday said, "but the people who dealt with him on an everyday basis in Seattle certainly could. The word is he was a whack job. Nobody up there was surprised when he shot himself."

"So," Gil said, "after all this time, we finally know that the same gun killed both men."

"It looks pretty solid that your frie—uh, this Spenser guy

killed that author. And Ms. Sanchez got sent up on a bum rap."

"Donovan did that," Gil said. "He took the easy way out."

"Well, that conviction is gonna be overturned and there are some Omaha people—judges, jury members, and especially Lieutenant Donovan—who are all gonna end up with egg on their faces. If I were you, I wouldn't be going back there anytime soon."

"No problem," Gil said.

Holliday closed his notebook. "Can I ask a question?"

"Sure. Anything."

"Why'd you do this? What do you get out of it?"

"It's a favor for a friend," Gil said.

"Are we talkin' acquaintance or friend now?" Holliday asked as he got up from the chair.

"Friend—definitely. Someone my wife and I owe our lives to."

Gil came back to the present, left the balcony, and started getting dressed for work. He remembered how grateful Wendell had been when he'd called that day to tell him Graciella had been cleared. He'd felt so good being able to do that for the man. What he still couldn't fathom, however, was why Wendell had stood by Graciella all those years, even to the point of going to Big Cedar with her. What was it that had bound them together so tightly for so long, in spite of Graciella's obvious disregard for Wendell as a man? Thankfully, he'd come to his senses in enough time to keep her from killing them.

Wendell Payne still couldn't believe it, even a whole year later. That nice Mr. Hunt had been able to get him a job in St. Louis at a big hotel downtown, a place that was grander than the one he'd worked at in Omaha. After Graciella was buried, he couldn't stay in that city anymore. Too many memories.

He left work that day as he usually did, drove to a small South St. Louis neighborhood, and pulled up in front of a brick building. A bell sounded, signaling dozens of children to run through the large doors, which had been propped open. One child, a small girl of about eight, waved and ran to the car. She opened the passenger's door and got in, smiling a gap-toothed smile.

"Hi, Daddy."

"Hi, baby girl. How was your day?"

"Okay."

"Just okay?"

"I got in a fight. Robert Pixley said something really mean and I punched him."

"Why did you do a thing like that?"

"He called me a bad name."

Wendell shook his head. "You got your momma's temper, baby. We got to work on that."

"Yes, Daddy."

"And how many times do I have to tell you?" he scolded gently. "Put your seat belt on when you get into the car, Gracie."

ACKNOWLEDGMENTS

Our sincere thanks to Tony Shill, the big kahuna at Big Cedar. And to his wonderful, cooperative staff: Debbie Bennett, Shari Beckley, and Sam Crockett. You were all so generous with your time and information, we hope we did your beautiful resort justice. And if we misplaced a lake, a tree, or a cabin, please forgive us.

A LOOK AT: EYE IN THE RING

BY ROBERT J. RANDISI

Miles Jacoby is torn between a career in the ring and his new ticket as a private investigator. When his sleuth mentor is murdered, it's bad enough that Miles's brother is charged. Worse, Miles finds himself in love with his brother's wife.

AVAILABLE NOW

ABOUT THE AUTHORS

Randisi was born and raised in Brooklyn, N.Y., and from 1973 through 1981 he was a civilian employee of the New York City Police Department, working out of the 67th Precinct in Brooklyn. After 41 years in N.Y, he now resides in Laughlin, NV, 90 miles South of Las Vegas, on the Colorado River, with his 25-year partner-in-life-and-crime, Marthayn Pelegrimas.

He is the author of the "Miles Jacoby," "Nick Delvecchio," "Joe Keough," and "Dennis McQueen," mystery series, and the co-author of the "Gil & Claire Hunt" series. He has been nominated four times for the Shamus Award from the Private Eye Writers of America, in the Novel and Short Story categories.

CHRISTINE MATTHEWS has published over sixty stories under her real name, Marthayn Pelegrimas, as well as her "Matthews" mystery pseudonym. She has appeared in *Alfred Hitchcock's Mystery Magazine, Deadly Allies II, Ellery Queen's Mystery Magazine, Lethal Ladies, For Crime Out Loud I & II, Mickey Spillane's Vengeance Is Hers, Cat Crimes On Holiday, Till Death Do Us Part, Hollywood and Crime* and *Crime Square*. Her stories have been chosen five times for Ed Gorman and Martin H. Greenberg's Best of the Year books, the most recent being the 2011 edition. She is the author of four novels and the editor of several anthologies.